Susan Yawn Tanner

Callahan
and the
Horses of
Hope

Secret Staircase Books

Cat Callahan Mysteries
by Rebecca Barrett and Susan Yawn Tanner

Callahan on the Case
Callahan and the Horses of Hope
Callahan's Christmas Feast (short story)
A Callahan Christmas (short story)

SUSAN YAWN TANNER

Callahan
and the
Horses of
Hope

Cat Callahan Mysteries, Book 2

Callahan and the Horses of Hope
Published by Secret Staircase Books, an imprint of
Columbine Publishing Group LLC
PO Box 416, Angel Fire, NM 87710

Book layout and design by Secret Staircase Books
Illustrations by Becky's Graphic Design, Svetlana Dubovetcaia,
Kalinin Dmitrii, lg0rzh, Zim235
First e-book edition: January, 2024
First paperback edition: January, 2024

An earlier version of this story was published in 2017 as
Trouble in Summer Valley
* * *

Publisher's Cataloging-in-Publication Data

Tanner, Susan Yawn
Callahan and the Horses of Hope / by Susan Yawn Tanner.
p. cm.
ISBN 978-1649141590 (paperback)
ISBN 978-1649141606 (e-book)

1. Cat Callahan (Fictitious character)—Fiction. 2. Southern
Mysteries—Fiction. 3. Amateur sleuths—Fiction. I. Title

Cat Callahan Mystery Series, Book 2.
Tanner, Susan Yawn, Cat Callahan Mysteries.

BISAC : FICTION / Mystery.

813/.54

To the older cousins who helped make my childhood a safe and happy place in those long-ago, lazy days of summer … Lewis, Bunt (aka William), Bill, and Bo (aka Kenneth). They were America's defenders and my heroes. They still are. And Catherine, first playmate, always remembered, forever missed.

Acknowledgement
For Marilyn Johnston, talented writer
(pen name cj petterson) and dear friend, who unceasingly supports and promotes my efforts to entertain through imagination and words.

Chapter 1

August in Alabama ... a washed-out blue sky, sweltering heat brewing the predictable afternoon storm. Right on cue thunder rumbles in the distance. That wimpy blue will soon darken to purple. The breeze shifts, and I catch the unmistakable scent of a fast-approaching storm. Bad luck for me. Forget that foolishness you hear that cats like a bath or will swim in a lake. It's all lies. Take it from me. I should know. I'm a cat. Callahan by name.

Why I thought it was a good idea to hitch a ride into town, I'll never know. It isn't proving to be my best scheme, but not even a cat can be brilliant every moment of every day. This small town doesn't have much to offer. A few of the restaurants look above average, which was unexpected. A miniature city-style park, complete with fountain and wrought iron benches, made a good place to rest my paws and catch forty winks. Otherwise, not much to see. It's cute, and all that, with an old-fashioned main street full of shops, but cute doesn't interest me. For the past thirty minutes, I've been stuck at the base of the courthouse steps, roasting in the heat still rising from the sidewalk while I wait for the gal who brought me to this party. Maybe a drenching wouldn't be the worst that could happen, after all.

It's mildly entertaining to people watch. And I might have dozed off for a bit. I've had company for the last little while, but the broad-shouldered man isn't much for small talk. He hasn't so much as shifted positions since he stepped from the dark pickup truck, sliding equally dark sunglasses into place all in one smooth move. The only interest I've seen him give his surroundings was a hard glance across the street at the motorcycle rider who sat pretty conspicuously on his bike. Even that interest faded when the brawny gentleman—and though I'm not one to judge by appearances, the term gentleman is a joke—fastened the strap on his helmet and went on his way.

After the smoke and the noise of the bike cleared, my guy in sunglasses leaned back against his truck once more. There's something about his manner that suggests his being here isn't by chance. I've given him more than a few sidelong looks, but there's been nothing more to see.

Abruptly, he straightens from his lazy position. Warned by his sudden movement, I turn, rewarded for my patience at last. There, far less fresh than when I arrived with her at nine on the dot this morning, is my ride back.

She looks more like the gal I've gotten used to seeing out and about at the ranch, although maybe a bit worse for wear at the moment. At some point, her dark hair escaped that neat pile she'd made on top of her head, and the slim fitting skirt she's wearing with a tucked-in blouse has a crease here and there. Other differences are more subtle and might be difficult for non-felines to detect, but they're clear to this street-smart, self-taught cat. Her eyes, pretty for a human, aren't filled *with anxiety as they were and her jaw isn't tight with tension. I'd say those changes signal a turn for the better in her circumstances.*

I'm glad not to see much of this morning's dread and anger when she was confronted at the base of these same steps by her 'significant other'—and who coined that ridiculous phrase, I wonder. They had a heated exchange when he insisted she would lose the battle ahead and suggested she cut her losses and sign the papers he waved in her face. If I'm any judge of circumstances and people—and I'm better than most—he was wrong.

It was clear to me that the man was already near desperation. If I'm right, he'll be even more desperate and might prove dangerous as well. Nothing I can't handle, but I'd prefer to hurry her along and avoid rather than engage.

Unfortunately, she doesn't look worried or rushed. There's a quiet confidence in her light movements as she descends toward me on black stiletto heels. These boardroom looks are at odds with the working horse ranch she owns and manages with a flair for the unusual. Of course, I haven't seen a lot of her so she could be manager in name only and gained those supple lines in a well-fitted home gym. Maybe, but I somehow don't think so.

* * *

Avery startled in surprise as the solidly built cat leapt lightly onto the step right below her feet. For a moment she doubted her eyes, that this could be the same cat that had accompanied her latest seasonal hire, but the golden eyes with that gray fur were as distinctive as those folded ears, the right one scarred. Prodded by the knowledge that Eddie would soon be emerging from the courthouse behind her, she sidestepped instead of stopping as she normally would have to let her fingers glide through the soft fur.

The cat surprised her, again, with a move that placed him firmly in her path. The movement was so precise it seemed almost intentional. Despite her haste and the remnants of dread that gripped her still, Avery allowed herself to smile and stooped to stroke the animal. "You *are* the cat that came here with the new guy, aren't you?" she murmured, as he arched in appreciation against her caress. Dax, it came to her after a moment. The man's name was Dax.

Golden-yellow eyes regarded her calmly but the sound of voices—angry male voices—had Avery quickly straightening her back. The thud of heavy footsteps warned her it was too late to turn her back and exit gracefully. She would look like a coward if she did that now and Avery was no coward. Knowing how fiercely Eddie hated cats, she swept him up in her arms. She had a quick vision of Eddie booting the innocent creature out of his path, if for no other reason than having seen her pet the animal.

Avery shifted to one side of the broad steps, giving plenty of room and silently willing Eddie to take his venom elsewhere. Her ex came down the stairs, his attorney following close at his heels. The attorney appeared as irritated as Eddie looked irate.

Eddie came to an abrupt halt inches away and Avery resigned herself to enduring one last ugly scene. Ugly was the best word she could give anything to do with Eddie these days. She marveled at the change the last five years had brought about in the man she'd once believed in and trusted completely. The handsome, energetic man at the height of a successful career had been replaced by this gaunt caricature of a person with poorly cut hair and ill-fitting clothes. She recognized the expensive taupe suit. She'd selected it for him, as she once had all of his clothing, and, at the time, it had fit his muscular shoulders to a tee.

"You won't win," he snarled at her.

Avery said nothing, knowing nothing she said would make any difference. Reminding him of the fact that she *had* won would do no good and would serve to fuel his resentment.

Paul Fletcher, once his closest friend and advisor and still his attorney, laid a hand on Eddie's shoulder. "Don't do this, Eddie. Let's get that coffee now."

Eddie ignored him, thrusting his face closer to Avery. She stood her ground, despite a tremor of alarm at the lack of control in his expression. She wouldn't let him see that it affected her. Her silence seemed to infuriate him even further. His pale face darkened with red blotches.

"Don't think this ends here."

She studied his face, seeing nothing left of the man she'd married. "It has ended," she said finally, quietly. "It's done, Eddie."

His harsh laugh had the cat tensing in her arms, and she instinctively snuggled him more closely to her chest.

"You stupid bitch! You would've been a hell of a lot smarter to take what I offered and gotten the hell out of Alabama. That ranch is mine, every acre, every horse."

She could see the hatred in his eyes where once she'd imagined she'd seen love. And she supposed Eddie could see with equal clarity the emptiness she felt when she looked at him.

"Over my dead body." She kept her voice steady by sheer strength of will. Her exhaustion was bone-deep. "The judge gave you twenty-four hours to remove the rest of your belongings from the ranch. Marla is welcome to continue on with me."

"Marla is my daughter, and that ranch is my property! Over your dead body?" he mimicked her words. His lips curled. "I hope you mean that, because that's just what I'm going to step over to take back what you've stolen from me."

"Eddie, what the hell…" Fletcher scrubbed a hand over his face in disgust.

Shock and fury hit Avery in a tidal wave of heat. "I can and will defend what's mine." Her voice was made hard by the reminder of all she'd been through, all he'd put her through. "You should listen to your attorney, Eddie. He might just keep you out of jail."

"Don't threaten me, you emasculating bitch."

Even more shocking than his threats, Eddie grabbed her shoulder, his fingers digging in so hard she sucked in her breath. As bad, as nasty, as things had gotten between them, Eddie had never laid hands on her—until now.

In one blurred moment, she sensed rather than saw the cat swipe unsheathed claws at the hand on her shoulder.

Eddie howled and jerked away with a string of curses more vulgar than anything she'd ever heard from him. He flung drops of blood from his hand, glaring at the thin line of welling blood before lunging forward. Avery couldn't tell if she or the cat were his target, but with the stair rail at her back she had nowhere to go.

Fletcher tried to restrain Eddie but his ineffectual attempt proved unnecessary. Before Avery had time for real fear, she watched in amazement as a complete stranger stepped past her, effortlessly pulling Eddie's arm behind his back so hard that Eddie's features contorted with pain rather than anger.

The man leaned in close and spoke with quiet effect. Avery wished she could hear the words that drained all resistance from Eddie's taut body. Eddie glared in disbelief then jerked backward as the other man loosened his grip.

The stranger turned his back on Eddie in dismissal. An assessing gaze skimmed Avery and the cat. "Mrs. Danson."

Avery was vaguely aware of Eddie stumbling past them, his attorney trailing behind.

"Ms. Wilson," she corrected automatically. She'd taken her own name back as soon as she'd filed for divorce more than a year ago. For a moment, she stared at him. His eyes were hidden by dark, aviator-style glasses, but she could almost feel his gaze, one that seemed as feline as the animal in her arms, but far more predatory, more in line with a panther than someone's pet.

"Ms. Wilson," he returned, without a hint of a smile. "I've been waiting for you. We need to talk."

Instinctively, Avery recoiled and shook her head. "No."

The man who had come to her rescue lifted an eyebrow, and she flushed at her own rudeness but she was exhausted, stretched to the limit.

"No," she said again, but with less force. "But thank you for your help."

"I understand your caution, however I've traveled a significant distance to meet with you."

"Meet with me? Who are you?" She felt completely bewildered by this turn of events. She'd been drained by the past few hours of courtroom drama and suspected she was far from her best, mentally. Even so, she knew she wasn't expecting a visitor of any kind, particularly not one with the authoritative air of the man standing in front of her. "What do you want with me?"

"This is not a sidewalk conversation." His tone brooked no argument. "Listen, it's late. You've got to eat and so do I. I need to talk with you, and it may as well be over food."

Whoever he was, Avery realized whatever he wanted to talk with her about, he wasn't going away until that happened.

* * *

Camp stood motionless during her silent study of him. He was a patient man, a hard-won virtue he hadn't possessed in his early years. There was no doubt in his mind his appearance screamed career military, even out of uniform. Short-clipped hair, deep brown edging toward gray. Navy polo tucked smoothly into pressed khakis. These days that persona, that image, infuriated and disgusted as often as it inspired. Since she had aligned her ranch with wounded veterans, he hoped at least for neutrality in that regard. He wondered if she sensed the concealed firearm he wore, if the knowledge of its existence would make her even more skittish.

He removed his sunglasses so that she could see his eyes. People often had a hard time trusting someone who wouldn't show their eyes, even if they didn't realize the cause of their mistrust. He'd had extensive training in human behavior, training that came in handy more often than not.

"I'm not selling my place, if that's what you're after. You won't be the first buyer Eddie has sent with an offer."

"I never laid eyes on your husband before today." Not in person, at any rate.

"I have animals to care for at home."

"You also need to eat." He suspected she'd missed more than one meal of late. A soft sigh seemed to release some of the tautness in her stance, and he pressed that advantage. "And a moment to catch your breath before you have to tackle your next challenge."

The slow widening of her eyes revealed the moment she accepted he knew far more about her than she did about him. "Who are you?"

"Food," he said firmly, taking her elbow but keeping a wary eye on the cat that had fended off Eddie Danson so handily. The cat, however, seemed to sense no threat in him. And there was none, at least no physical threat. "There's a restaurant down the block. You'll be surrounded by people, and hopefully we can find an unobtrusive place for your cat."

At his words, she gave the cat one last stroke then placed him gently at her feet. The move pulled her arm from Camp's light hold. "I'd love to have him but he's not mine." As if to prove her point, the cat wound once around her legs, then trotted gracefully up the steps and disappeared into the foliage.

Straightening, she met his stare fully, and Camp felt a quick jolt of unexpected and unwanted attraction. Looking into those eyes was a little like looking into a forest. At first glance, a person would catch the myriad swirl of greens and browns with flecks of gold before their gaze adjusted sufficiently to see the depths buried below.

Camp glanced away. She was an assignment. And pretty eyes, like a pretty face, could hide a wealth of evil. He slid his hand under her elbow once more. He expected her to shrug him off. She didn't, but she didn't yield to his light pressure either. It was more as if she ignored or didn't notice. Not being a ladies' man by nature, the fact was more a curiosity to him than a disappointment.

The walk was brief and silent. Camp's gaze scanned the sidewalks on both sides of the quaint, paved street with its old-fashioned parking meters, boutique shops, and numerous restaurants.

"This isn't quite the rural town I expected."

Her lips curved. "Casino nearby. We capitalized on that like everything else that comes our way."

We. He picked up on the nuance as he held open the door of the little café that boasted French cuisine. He'd been dubious of that claim but now wondered if he'd judged the restaurant too quickly. He'd made note of the casino in the files downloaded to his laptop but hadn't thought of the cultural impact upon the small town. "You've lived here a while."

"Yes, I have." She didn't elaborate and he didn't press. He'd studied the facts and figures of her life, but interesting though they were, they'd been nothing compared to the vibrancy he sensed below the surface calm she presented now.

Their hostess was young, with smooth hair and wide, deep blue eyes. She was at least twenty years his junior, and the flirtatious glance she gave him would've been amusing if Avery Wilson hadn't noticed it as well. Her husband, he recalled reading, had been fond of late nights with very young women.

"We'd like a table by a window," he told their hostess. If it were cooler, he would have chosen the sidewalk area with its hanging ferns and scrolled iron railing around the perimeter, but he suspected even the wide blades of the overhead fans couldn't hold the heat at bay. Nor was he certain the thunderstorm rumbling in the distance would remain distant.

Seated in an alcove filled with soft light from both the sheer-curtained window and a small but elegant crystal chandelier, Camp ordered iced tea and Avery asked for water with lemon. After a day in court, Camp wouldn't have been surprised if she had selected from the wine menu.

He was intrigued, even a little impressed, when she sat watching him with that fathomless regard, waiting for him to speak. She didn't lean against the back of the cushioned chair but kept herself slightly forward, alert. Although he could see her fatigue, that direct gaze never wavered. Patience in this woman, he thought. Patience and strength. He acknowledged the allure of that combination, made himself put it aside. It was altogether likely that his investigation would not turn out well for her.

He handed her a menu but she set it to one side. "You wanted to talk, and my time is limited."

Unruffled, he glanced at his menu as they were served their drinks and ordered a simple meal of salad and grilled white fish for both of them.

He could feel her scrutiny, but when he looked up, her expression was a careful blank. If she was irritated by his high-handedness in ordering for her, it was well-hidden.

As the waitress walked away with their order, Camp removed a small fold of leather from his back pocket and withdrew two cards. Silently he handed her his credentials. One was his military ID. The other was styled as a business card with his bogus position and responsibilities. The latter had been created and printed a little more than a week earlier.

He watched her face as she studied them. Not until those truly incredible eyes lifted to gaze into his, did he speak. "You applied for the wounded veteran program. Equine therapy."

Her eyes widened with what could be either excitement or trepidation.

"Lieutenant Colonel Kirkland. I'd given up," she admitted. "I knew the government moved slowly but …" She gave a little lift of her shoulders.

Camp schooled his expression, not sure where this was headed but prepared to follow whatever lead came his way. "Your application crossed my desk about eighteen months ago," he prompted.

"I didn't mean to insult you or imply you were the hold-up, but I did expect someone sooner."

Which gave away exactly nothing, he thought. He found it interesting that she toyed with the elegant black napkin which had been folded around the place setting. He also noted that there was no pale circle around her slender finger. She hadn't waited until the divorce was final to remove her wedding ring. From what he'd read of her husband, he couldn't say he blamed her.

"We do eventually get to every applicant."

He lost the opportunity to judge her response to his words as their waitress arrived with their salads. By the time they were alone again, she'd resumed her watchful pose. He gave a mental shrug, perfectly willing to retrieve the gauntlet he'd tossed and she'd ignored.

He picked up his fork and waited for her to do the same before he spoke again. "When would be a good time for me to tour your facilities? Do you need a day or two to regroup?"

She blinked. "Regroup?"

"I assume this morning's court appearance was successful given your husband's—ex-husband's—reaction but it must still have been difficult."

"Difficult describes the last few years. This morning?" She shook her head. "I'll take a few hours drama in exchange for peace."

"What will you do with that peace?" The question, he was honest with himself, had less to do with his purpose in being there than with the woman.

She didn't answer right away, and, for a while, he thought she wouldn't at all.

"Be me."

She didn't elaborate, and he realized she didn't need to add anything, not for her or for him. Those two simple words were very revealing. He wondered if she realized just how revealing. What kind of a lie had her marriage imposed on her existence? And would that lie figure into his investigation?

Realizing she had said all she would, he leaned back in his chair. He had to focus on the business at hand.

"Tell me about the horses you use in your veteran assistance program." His word choice was deliberate. Use. Not plan to use. They both knew that no veterans had been referred yet. Would she correct his word choice? Would it mean anything if she didn't?

"My horses?" she asked. "I could talk about them forever. They all love what they do. They know their job and they love doing it."

Was her wording adroit? Or was it meaningless?

She didn't remind him that she was still waiting for the first veteran to arrive at her facility, didn't explain or apologize for funds sent but not earned. Camp put away his disappointment, reminding himself that ignoring a misstatement wasn't self-incrimination, and listened to the soft Southern cadence of her voice. He'd lived in so many places over the course of his career, in and out of the States, that he himself had a diction that could have placed him anywhere and nowhere, depending upon the language he chose to employ.

Her eyes brightened as she described the animals, one by one, rarely noting bloodlines—some of which he already knew were impressive—focusing instead on their personality and backstory. How they came to her and how she felt about them seemed far more important than their sires and dams.

"I know what rescue animals are, of course, but is a *kill* pen as ugly as the name implies?"

Sorrow, and something he suspected was anger, touched her features. "Uglier. And sometimes I hear about horses with great potential too late. I have contacts at several facilities who do what they can for the animals. I wish I could take them all, but there are other people besides me who help save as many as possible."

"How do they end up there? I saw a news report once that implied most of them were vicious killers."

"That's not true. Yes, some are mistreated to the point they strike back, but most?" She shook her head. "Animals are an investment of time, income, and energy. Too many people realize that too late and throw them away like so much trash. And then, there are horses injured in competitive sports that need healing time and others too old to continue competition. Their owners don't want to be bothered feeding and caring for them as they heal or age. They just move on to the next new toy. These are the ones I can almost always take and train and make into a useful instructor horse. Some, who've been abused, I find I can't help at all."

"What then? I'm certain you don't send them back where they came from."

"No. Never." She sighed. "There are a few rescue farms in the area that take them when they can, but I also have a pasture full of horses that are nothing but an expense."

"Of the ones who have worked out for you, do you have a favorite?"

"Jack," she said without hesitation. "He was a hunter-jumper and one of my first finds for New Hope Ranch. He has papers a mile long, but he was injured early in his career and his owners no longer had any use for him. He was a stallion, which is pretty rare in a successful working competitor, but so gentle. If he'd made it to some big stakes' wins, I never would have gotten him. He would've been put to stud. It took him a year to heal and another year to learn what I needed from him. The amazing thing with Jack is that he is a producer, and his offspring are equally talented, equally gentle. I've been offered a small fortune for any one of them, but they aren't for sale. From time to time, I do let rescues go to other homes in order to make room for more, but they don't leave me unless I think they're needed someplace more and I can be sure they'll be well-treated. And even then, there will be stipulations to the transfer."

"Stipulations?"

"If they're no longer wanted or can't be cared for where they are, they'll come back to me."

He raised his brows at that. "Could get expensive for

you if you've already added more to your herd."

"I'm pretty good at vetting potential new owners. None have come back so far." Her quick grin held an appeal he didn't expect and found uncomfortable. Her expression turned somber as she added, "And if they do, I'll make a way for them. Always."

He kept her talking with a well-placed question or two, listening as intently for nuances to her words as he did to the humor of her interspersed anecdotes about the animals she loved. He found himself hoping she was everything she seemed, if only for the sake of the animals depending upon her. She was either very clever or had absolutely nothing to hide.

Conversation flowed easily throughout their entrée and he realized he was disappointed when she placed her fork aside. She'd finished only half of what was on her plate when she laid her napkin on the tablecloth.

"Thank you for the meal. Truly. I have to get back to take care of things, but you're welcome to come out anytime. I cancelled classes today so my instructors won't be there. Tomorrow would be more helpful to you."

"You have guest quarters?" He asked it as a question although he already knew the answer.

He found her momentary hesitation interesting.

"We do," she admitted, "but it isn't prepared for guests. There's a guest cabin—the one my ex-husband was using— but it hasn't been deep-cleaned in several months although we keep the cooling and heating on so it's aired."

Her voice trailed away as if to give him an opportunity to offer to stay in town.

When he remained silent, she sighed. "I guess I could bring some towels and linens out but you'd be *much* more comfortable in one of the hotels in town. There are several that are more than nice."

He leaned back in his chair, every instinct heightened. She most definitely did not want him staying on her property.

"I don't need much to be comfortable," he said, "and it will be easier for me to see what I need to see if I'm there during various times of the day."

She frowned. "You plan a lengthy stay?"

"It will take some time to evaluate everything I need to review."

As her frown deepened, Camp wished he hadn't felt such a swift initial attraction to her. It was almost certain to be a feeling that could go nowhere.

Chapter 2

Campbell Kirkland paid the tab, and they walked through the dusk back to the courthouse parking lot. The energy Avery had felt as she talked about her horses had faded and exhaustion seeped back into her until it was the familiar dead weight she'd known since things had gone so very wrong with her marriage. It felt like forever since she'd been able to rest, to relax her guard. Not since this fight had started, not since she realized there *was* a fight. She'd won but she didn't fool herself. Despite her words to Eddie, she knew it wasn't over. He wasn't going to go away. Maybe someday, but not yet.

As they walked, a slow sense of dread blended with the exhaustion. Along with threatening her over the course of their long, drawn-out court fight, he'd threatened the horses as well. They meant nothing to him, now, except as a means to an end and that end was money. Always money. For newer cars, nicer clothes. For gambling. She'd realized too late the siren call that dice and cards held for him. Not to mention the women, always younger than her. When had *she* stopped being enough for him?

The carefully preserved oaks, so pretty by day, seemed to crowd the sidewalk with shadows. She experienced a sudden sense of urgency, a feeling she should have gone straight home.

Avery heard Camp's growl of anger before she saw her SUV. She wasn't surprised by the shattered glass of her windshield. She wasn't even surprised to see the gray cat with those odd, folded ears pacing the sidewalk beside the slashed tires. She had, she realized, almost been expecting ... something.

* * *

Well, I hope these two enjoyed their grub for the games have begun, and I haven't eaten since lunch, which wasn't bad, but I burned that energy long ago.

Unless I miss my guess, which doesn't happen all that often, this horse gal is going to assume that her nasty ex-husband is the culprit. She might could handle him well enough ... at least with my help ... but he may not be all we're up against. Sure, a blade of some kind slashed those tires but it wasn't a knife that shattered that glass. I'd bet Dax's last dollar there's a bullet somewhere behind that ruined glass. I'd also bet it was discharged from a gun with a silencer. Otherwise, we'd have a crowd surrounding us. Ex-husband, maybe, maybe not. I'm thinking this is a step above his current mental capacity.

Too bad these two don't yet have a clue how smart I am. They'll catch on; the humans always do, but it takes a nudge here and there. Sometimes a really strong nudge.

* * *

"I'll call the police." Camp, as he'd told her to call him, pulled his phone from his pocket.

"I can't wait for them. I've got to get home," Avery said, staring at her ruined SUV. "Now! You've got to take me."

She blessed the fact that he didn't argue. He took one glance at her face and gestured toward a dark gray truck parked close to hers. Before they took more than a step or two, however, the cat snagged a paw in Camp's trousers, then sat down and stared up at him intently.

When Camp stepped forward again, his pants were snagged again. When he stopped, the cat sat. "Okay." Camp hesitated. His expression said clearly that he felt more than a little stupid for talking to a cat. "What?"

The cat stood and stalked back to Avery's SUV. Camp looked at Avery. "Your cat wants to show us something."

"You're crazy. He's not my cat. And I have to get home!" Avery knew her voice had risen slightly with each short statement.

"Two minutes," Camp answered, and he followed the cat back to her SUV.

Avery trailed after him, fighting a sense of panic and tears. Crying wouldn't help, it never had, never would, and she'd given it up long ago. Panic didn't change things either, she knew, but the tears were easier to quell than this horrific sense that something terrible was going to happen to things that truly mattered. If it hadn't already.

Camp made a closer study of the windshield, studying the broken glass. He whistled softly. "Does your ex own a gun?"

"Eddie? Absolutely not. He hates guns, though I own several. Are you saying … ?"

She stepped closer, trying to see what Camp was studying.

"I'm saying you have a problem." He opened the door to the vehicle, quickly finding the entry and exit for the bullet that went through her front seat. Avery waited numbly while he continued his search in the back seat and pocketed two bullets. "I'll get these to the police later. Let's go."

He turned with an odd expression to the cat who had observed him from the hood of the car without moving. "Interesting."

Camp didn't seem any more surprised than she when the cat leapt lightly into his truck with them and settled on the console.

"Let's go, then." He started the engine, and Avery put her head against the headrest, anxious to be home but terrified of what she might find when she got there.

She listened as Camp made a series of phone calls. With each one he was careful to tell the person on the other end that they were on his truck speakerphone. First the sheriff's office, giving brief, pertinent facts of what they'd found, of Avery's concern for the safety of her property. He affirmed they were on their way to the ranch and gave the address without glancing at her. Even the awareness that he had it memorized couldn't edge past her growing anxiety sufficiently to make her question the fact. The next call seemed to be to a travel agency canceling a flight for later in the week. And then one so cryptic she couldn't tell if it was to friend or family or someone he barely knew. Nothing seemed to be in whole sentences and the sentence fragments could have meant anything.

Although the distance to her property wasn't great, the change from town to country was abrupt and complete. Within minutes, stately homes with manicured lawns gave way to long, rolling hills. The headlights of his truck swept field after white-fenced field. All familiar to her and dearly-loved.

He drove smoothly, expertly, and very, very fast, for which she was grateful, especially if it was in deference to her anxiety to be home. She supposed a military man might be expected to be obedient to speed limits. She was glad he wasn't, at least for this trip.

Again, she didn't miss the fact that he didn't need to ask directions and turned without hesitation into her drive. On some level that bothered her, on another she'd almost expected it.

She would've preferred that Camp's initial glimpse of the ranch happened in the light of morning. She'd worked hard, poured her very heart and soul into it, and she knew it was impressive at first sight, but he'd see little of its beauty in the dark. She wanted him to be impressed, to approve her application to provide equine therapy to wounded veterans, but nothing mattered in this moment as much as knowing her horses were there and unharmed.

As the truck skimmed along the lengthy drive, she realized every light blazed from all three stable areas. Her heart stuttered in her chest.

She was almost nauseous by the time Camp had the engine off and was barely aware of him coming around the hood to open her door as she stumbled out without waiting. Kicking off her heels, she took off toward the barn at a run, leaving Camp to follow—Camp and the cat.

* * *

The sound of weeping was clear in the evening air. Avery felt the blood freeze in her veins well before she reached the huge sliding barn door, standing wide in a manner that was not the norm for this time of day. She believed that horses, like humans, thrived on a set routine for meals and rest. Blessedly the days of having to give riding lessons at odd hours to adjust to her clients' work and school schedules were well in the past for her.

Before she reached the opening, a shadow pushed away from the side of the barn. The light from the barn crossed the man's face in the same moment she heard the cat give a soft greeting.

"Dax?"

He jerked his chin toward the barn. "The young lady wouldn't let me help. She told me to go away. I couldn't feel good about leaving her, crying and all, so I waited for you."

"Is she hurt?" That was Avery's first thought and greatest concern.

Dax shook his head, his gaze shifting from her to Camp who'd walked up to stop beside her. "Doesn't seem to be, but she's got a gun. I'm not sure that's such a good thing." He turned his attention to the cat. "Callahan, hey, I wondered where you were." He glanced at Avery, "Unless you need me, I'll turn in."

"I've got it from here, but thank you," Avery said and watched as the man disappeared into the dark. The cat didn't follow.

Taking a deep breath, she walked into the barn, mindful of Camp at her side. The sight of Marla sitting against a stall door, head in hands, nearly stopped her heart and her steps slowed even more. In a smooth movement, Camp retrieved the gun from the floor at her feet then stepped back as Avery crouched in front of her.

She touched her stepdaughter's hair lightly. "Marla, are you hurt?"

Marla looked up at her with tear-drenched eyes and shook her head, but dropped it again without saying anything more.

Seeing no sign of injury or trauma, Avery forced herself to rise and move past Marla to the first stall. She drew her first breath of relief as her beloved Jack thrust his head over the stall door and nickered at her. She caressed his broad forehead and moved on, one stall at a time, one barn at a time, relief growing as she was greeted by every animal in turn. She touched each as she passed, quickly, lightly, reassuring herself they were unharmed, and that all was well. With them at least. The same was not true of her stepdaughter.

Turning, she hurried back to the weeping Marla, already knowing that Eddie had come and gone. Camp was crouched in front of Eddie's daughter, but she had turned her face from him. Her stepdaughter was a private person, and she wouldn't appreciate having a stranger see her in an emotional state of any kind. Avery dropped to her knees beside Marla, aware and grateful when Camp discreetly withdrew to one side.

"Hey, what's going on?" She kept her voice calm, though she was anything but calm inside. Despite knowing her horses were safe, her nerves jangled from the events of the day—the scene with Eddie and the damage to her vehicle—and now dismay at the realization that something had gone terribly wrong here as well. Marla despised tears, never willingly cried.

Marla turned to her, eyes as blue as Eddie's and long, dark lashes that never needed mascara, drenched with tears, as others streamed down her face. "Oh, Avery, I'm so sorry. I tried to stop him. He was wild, absolutely crazy with fury."

Avery's stomach clenched. "Are you hurt?"

Marla shook her head vehemently. "No, of course not. He'd never hurt me. He's my father." But Avery realized her voice didn't carry as much conviction as it once would have.

"Then what happened? What did he do?" She couldn't bring herself to so much as say Eddie's name.

Dropping her head, Marla waved a hand toward the tack room where they stored bridles, always in meticulous order and cleanliness.

As Avery stepped to the doorway, she couldn't stop her gasp. Dozens of valuable headstalls, fully tacked out with bits and reins, were heaped in the middle of the floor, costly leather slashed in half.

"I tried to stop him. I did," Marla's voice carried softly from the hallway. "He screamed at me and shoved me away like I was nothing to him." Marla's voice held equal tones of sorrow and anxiousness. "I'm not sure he even knew it was me talking, begging him to stop. He kept saying you had to pay, over and over." Marla stopped abruptly, as if stricken by what she was admitting about her own father.

With a sigh, Avery turned resolutely away from the

carnage. The bridles could be replaced. Her horses were safe, and Marla was unharmed, though shaken by the scene with Eddie.

She returned to stand in front of Marla and held out her hand. Slowly, Marla took it and rose gracefully to her feet. She was taller than Avery, but not by much, and their eyes met. "I'm sorry, Avery. So very sorry."

"This isn't your fault, Marla. I don't hold you accountable in the least."

"Would it be better," her voice broke slightly, but she took a breath and finished, "better for you … easier … if I left?" Marla appeared uncharacteristically young and vulnerable, far from her usual shoulders-back confidence.

"Is that what you want?" Avery kept her words calm even as an added stress slammed through her. Marla was her right hand. She couldn't imagine how she'd ever replace her; how she could possibly find someone as reliable and as committed to helping New Hope Ranch succeed. Even harder was the thought of losing Marla as a part of her personal life. They were family. But Avery knew she had to do the right thing. Eddie's daughter was clearly caught in the middle. "Would it be easier on you? I know these last years have been as difficult for you as they have for me. I'd make sure you were okay financially if you feel that's best for you."

"No." Marla's expression was one of pure shock at the suggestion. "I never want to leave here. This is my home. We've built everything from nothing." Her lips quivered. "Me and you. Together."

Avery released the breath she'd been holding, acknowledging a familiar wave of affection. She and Marla were a good team, had been from the beginning. "Well, that's that then." She smiled, though she didn't yet feel like smiling. "We'll get through this like we have the rest. Your father will get a grip eventually and move on. He loves you, Marla, whatever he said about or to you, it will be okay."

Marla shook her head, and her mid-length layers of hair swirled slightly with the movement. "You didn't see him, Avery. I'm not sure he can pull himself together. His hands were shaking—not trembling—but shaking hard, and he was talking wild. Kept saying *they* would be angry, and he wasn't going to take the blame for what you'd done to him."

"They?" Avery was completely confused. "They, who?"

"I don't know. I asked. He wouldn't answer me."

"Don't worry about it for now," Avery said firmly, shifting into mother mode. "You're exhausted and so am I. We'll get some rest and clean up this mess first thing in the morning. I'll lock up here. You go on inside."

Marla didn't seem at all sure about leaving Avery and turned her attention to Camp for the first time. Her eyes narrowed in warning. "Who are you?"

Camp gave his name and held out his hand, waiting patiently for Marla to shake it. Avery could see her hesitance and offered as much explanation as she could.

"Mr. Kirkland will be staying in the guest quarters while he checks out what we can offer wounded veterans." She was relieved to see Marla's shoulders lose some of their tension.

"Welcome to New Hope Ranch," Marla said, with more welcome but still no smile.

Avery suspected she didn't have much *smile* left in her after the episode with her father. "Get some rest, Marla," she said gently. "I'll get Mr. Kirkland settled and see you in the morning. Everything will seem better with the sun."

Marla gave her an *I'm not so sure* look but she complied, giving Avery a light, quick hug before turning to leave. At the door of the barn, she cast a final, anxious glance back at Avery.

"She's worried about you," Camp offered when she was gone.

Avery sighed. "Well, that's two of us." She brushed tangled hair from her face. "I'll show you to the guest quarters and let you take your bags in while I get some fresh linen."

"What remains to be done out here?"

The question surprised her. "With the horses? Nothing." She glanced toward the tack room with the tangle of ruined headstalls. "Nothing at all."

* * *

Well, well, now, isn't that interesting? Avery Wilson doesn't look old enough to be playing mom to a young woman of Marla's age, and I doubt that she is. But the relationship seems to work for the two of them. And, of course, in terms of physical age, it's plausible.

There's a heck of a lot to be done in short order but not tonight. All I need for now is a meal and a rest. My buddy, Dax, will see to it that I get both.

I make my way out to the clearing where we share a pup tent. For the record, the moniker for our shelter doesn't mean there's a canine involved and I'm grateful there isn't. Dax explained ... yeah, he talks to me, sometimes a lot, sometimes not so much ... that soldiers wear dog tags and are always yipping about something so where they sleep might as well be called a pup tent. But then I heard him tell someone else the army is a dog's life and that gave the tent its name.

In any case, it all sounds darned unpleasant to me.

Dax seems to feel a kinship with some of the folks we've seen come here to ride the ranch horses. He doesn't talk to them but I've noticed him take his morning and afternoon break in the shade of a tree while he watches. I may get to stick around to help this set of humans stop the ex's harassment and figure out if there's more than him to what's going on. It sounds possible with the mention of some mysterious they *who are going to hold him accountable for some mysterious something.*

For the moment, however, first, food, and then sleep.

Chapter 3

Avery was an early riser by nature, on top of which she'd not rested well. Even after her body had demanded she be in bed, her mind had skittered among worry over her horses, hope that she was handling things well with Marla, and trepidation over the arrival of Camp Kirkland in the midst of this mess. Long before first light, she was at her computer, coffee mug in hand. She'd intended to do some research on him, the same as she did on any students or potential students who came her way, particularly those whose needs originated in trauma of some sort. It was essential that she always know what she was up against in her efforts to help her clients, sometimes to do no more than reach them, to connect with them. Added to that, she was careful to accept clients she thought would benefit most from what she had to offer and never those whose past indicated they would be a menace to her animals or her team.

She also had to read through more of the financial documents that Marla sent her without fail. Avery had given Marla complete authority to execute purchase orders and pay bills, but she refused to finalize any transaction that Avery had not first reviewed and blessed. Marla was careful to include a summary, telling her what documents were attached and what response was needed. Avery never let her know that she sometimes did no more than skim the summary and forward her e-mail approval for the contents. Marla was an absolute genius when it came to all things financial. Far be it from Avery to second-guess the rock-solid choices Marla made in how and when to spend their resources above and beyond the necessities of feed and supplements, vaccinations and de-wormer, routine dental, and—always—the farrier.

Checking her e-mail before she did anything else was now more habit than necessity. There was a time, when she was first starting out, that checking daily—often multiple times a day—for potential new clients was a must. She couldn't afford to miss any inquiry in the early days. Now, she was flooded with clients. All came to her by word of mouth. New Hope Ranch did not, and did not need to, advertise.

"I think I need more coffee," she murmured. Snooping into Mr. Kirkland's existence could wait, as could the next several dozen e-mails. Ranch business, like Marla's correspondence, came before anything else, and those, at least, were out of the way.

Coffee and fresh air, both would help to clear her head. She stepped out of the well-appointed kitchen, rarely used these days, to the wrap-around porch. Cup in hand, she sank into a cushioned wicker chair, letting the early morning coolness wash over her.

Before she had time to relax completely, her cell phone rang and she wasn't surprised to see the sheriff's name displayed. His daughter had been one of her first students. Long before she'd ever dreamed of her own place, she had been a riding instructor at a fairly large, local riding school. She'd learned enough to know she could make it in the business. She and the Farleys had remained friends.

"What the hell, Avery?"

Little as she felt like laughing, she couldn't help herself. "Good morning, Ben. What the hell, indeed. I take it you've seen my vehicle."

"Seen it, combed through it, and had it towed. You'll get it back when it's fixed, but we're not done with it yet. Do I need to bust Eddie's ass?"

"I wish." She sighed. "But you can't, Ben, and we both know it. Eddie may have slashed the tires but you'll never prove it. And he doesn't own a gun."

"That you know of."

"Oh, Ben, come on. You know he doesn't carry."

"What I know is he's not the man he once was or the man I thought he was. We can't be sure what he would and wouldn't do at this point. You watch yourself, Avery. Watch yourself and I'll watch him."

Avery's throat tightened. So many good people here, so many who cared about her. And a hell of a way to be reminded of that, a tiny voice chimed in. She ignored it.

For a brief moment, she considered telling him about the destruction Eddie had wreaked upon some extremely expensive tack. The thought of Marla being questioned about her exchange with her father, of Marla's comments being a factor if Ben decided to arrest Eddie, deterred her. She would not pit daughter against father. She thanked the sheriff, and he rang off, reiterating that he'd have her vehicle towed to a repair shop and returned to her as soon as their investigation allowed.

Avery didn't put much faith in that investigation but she didn't say so. Not that Ben Farley wasn't as smart as any big city sheriff, but it'd be a long shot if he managed to pin it on Eddie, even as convinced as he was that Eddie was guilty.

She, however, wasn't convinced. Eddie might be brave enough and cowardly enough to slash a set of tires, but bullets, no, not so much. Truth be told, if anyone could figure out what had happened, she'd put more faith in Camp Kirkland than the local law enforcement. Even with that, she hoped he wouldn't be around long enough to solve any mysteries for her or anyone else. She wanted him to see what he needed to see and go back to whoever needed to hear it and declare New Hope Ranch more than adequate for the veteran equine therapy program. She had her heart set on it and would have been even more frustrated by the long delay if the drawn-out fight with Eddie hadn't taken so much of her time and energy.

Her gaze was pulled by her thoughts to the guest bungalow where she'd put Camp for the night and likely for the duration of his visit. She wasn't surprised to see a light already on. His air of confidence and authority was appealing. She could acknowledge the fact while also accepting she wouldn't allow herself to be attracted to him for that or any other reason, like strong hands and broad shoulders. She'd once found Eddie's strong hands and broad shoulders just as appealing. See where that had gotten her. She shook off the thought, determined not to go there. It was time to move forward, and forward was showing Mr. Kirkland that she had a perfectly viable program, medically approved to help veterans regain some sense of normalcy and control of their own destiny. The medically approved part he should already know even if all he'd done was skim the surface of her application. But the viable part—that much she could *and would* demonstrate to his satisfaction.

By the time her first client had arrived—she refused to call or even think of them as patients—Avery had downed another cup of coffee with two slices of whole wheat toast, showered and pulled her hair back and up with a clip. She would have preferred to forgo makeup completely, but her mirror said otherwise. She refused to go about appearing wan and dreary, like some heroine in a tragedy. The judge's ruling had averted the tragedy she'd feared; there could be no heroine without a hero, and Eddie was no hero. The last thought brought a glimmer of a smile as she brushed the slightest bit of color onto her cheeks.

She waited for their eight o'clock client at the first paddock. Rob had been weeks away from his high school graduation when a car crash had taken his closest friend and left him with debilitating injuries. He'd been referred to her by a neurosurgeon who believed Rob's own mind was deliberately holding him back from fullest recovery. He'd been driving when the accident occurred. The parents of the deceased had forgiven their son's friend, but Rob couldn't or wouldn't forgive himself.

He'd come to the ranch a young man with everything in life ahead of him, but wanting nothing more than the one thing life couldn't offer. A second chance for his friend. Slowly the horses were giving Rob a second chance … at happiness. Rob greeted her, now, with a shy smile. That smile had taken weeks to surface but Avery didn't credit herself. It was Rob's bond with Mr. BoJangles—or Jangle as he'd come to be called—that had brought about the slow change in him.

The youngest of her instructors, Leanne, brought Jangle to the paddock and stood waiting patiently in the center for Rob to come to her.

Avery remained at the paddock opening as Rob walked slowly but with increasing steadiness across the soft smooth dirt of the paddock.

"Why didn't she bring the horse to him?" Camp's voice came from behind her.

Avery turned slowly. "You're very quiet on your feet." It wasn't *quite* an accusation.

"Habit. Training. Sorry, it wasn't intentional."

But she wondered if that were true. He was here, after all, to scrutinize everything about her. The thought should have bothered her, she supposed, but she had to be glad when the government cared enough about the men and women who had served and been injured for their service to see that they received good care. She had reason to know that wasn't always the case and not just because of the bombardment of bad press about veteran aid. She was still angry at how long it had taken for her brother to get the help he needed and, even then, it had been too little, too late.

Pulling her thoughts back to Camp's question, she said, "Rob came to us six months ago in a wheelchair. He had to *want* to walk before he could *relearn* to walk. Jangle has a way about him that makes people want to come to him. Leanne is smart enough to use that fact to full advantage."

When Camp didn't answer, she turned to look at him and found he was watching the young man and the horse. Jangle never took his wide, dark eyes off Rob despite the slow process, never shook his head in impatience. Avery felt the moment Camp realized that Leanne had stepped away and solid training alone held the animal quietly in position. Avery knew it was more than training. Jack's offspring—and Jangle was the oldest of them—seemed to understand intuitively the needs of the humans who came into their care. When Rob reached Jangle's side, the large animal lowered his head to the young man's chest. Arms, not as strong as they surely once were, but stronger every day, circled the horse's neck. Leanne came forward with a two-step stool and stood by, ready to assist, but not offering help that wasn't needed, as Rob slowly stepped up and into the saddle. He gave Leanne another brief smile then gathered the reins and began to guide Jangle slowly around the paddock as Leanne retrieved the stool and moved away.

Avery beckoned Leanne forward and introduced her to Camp. "Leanne is in charge of Barn One."

She'd thought that Camp would question Leanne, but all he did was give his name and say that he was there on behalf of the wounded veterans program. When Leanne returned to the center of the ring to keep careful watch over Rob's and Jangle's progress, Camp asked, "What does *in charge of* mean? Does she have a title?"

Avery nodded. "She's Barn Manager. That's what is on the books. Reality is so much more. She is in charge of the horses in her barn—there are six in each—and the clients matched to those horses. The horses are hers to manage as far as exercise, feed, training, leisure time. Whatever they need, she ensures they have. When they are with a client, her focus is on that client and that horse the entire time. She must know the medical history of each client, understand their primary doctor's instructions for their therapy. Each barn has an indoor and an outdoor paddock. She's tasked with knowing when the ground needs to be worked or even altered in some way. Of recognizing when maintenance is needed and making it happen."

She wasn't surprised by Camp's raised brow. "One person? All that?"

"One person. All that and more. She doesn't *do* it all mind you, but she knows the why and manages the how and the when. The *and more* is that each barn has a part-time barn helper who cleans the stalls, makes sure water tubs are clean and horses are all fed according to Leanne's specific direction for each. They also learn to drive a tractor and work the ground if they feel comfortable doing that. She's also responsible for their performance and development as employees."

"Has she been here long?"

"Almost five years. Leanne came to me straight from graduation … physical therapy. She didn't want to work in a hospital or clinic. She loves horses and she loves people."

"Does she live here? Do any of your barn managers? You have three barns so three managers, right?"

"That's right, and Leanne did live here for a while … in the guest house where you're staying. She married a couple of years ago and she and her husband bought a small property not far from here. One of my requirements is that my barn managers must be within a thirty-minute commute at the most. Now the bungalow is back to its original purpose—a haven for clients who need a place to *be* for a little while."

"This isn't just a job for them, is it?"

Avery gave him a quick glance, realizing that he truly got it. "My team? No. It can't be. Not for them to be successful. It's a career plus a lifestyle. Like the military is for some."

She started to walk toward Barn Two. The first appointment for that barn was another thirty minutes out. Camp followed as she expected he would.

"Why three barns? Why not one big one?"

Her answer wasn't quick or flippant, because it was actually a good question. "In the beginning, it was because I started small. I had the first six of my horses to work with and not a great deal of savings or income. I had that first barn built just large enough to house those six because it was as much as I could afford at the time. After I put in the outdoor paddock at one end and the covered paddock at the other, the setup worked so well that I did the same with Barn Two rather than adding on to what was there."

Camp nodded. "Makes sense."

"As we grew larger, we housed the horses by their skillsets matched to our clients. The horses in Barn One provide therapy for clients who have been injured, like Rob. Leanne is good with the grief and the anger and the frustration that comes with all of that—the loss of what they had, the fight to get it back."

"What about Barn Two?" Camp asked quietly. "Who is that for?"

"Children born with disabilities, whose parents or caregivers of some sort are smart enough, care enough, and brave enough to want them to have more, to have and be everything they can. They choose horses, choose *us*, to give it to them."

Camp heard the passion in her voice, heard the caring. But caring didn't always equate to ethics, he knew. He almost hated to push on through the questioning. Not that he had a choice. The questioning and the digging were why he'd been sent.

"And Barn Three?"

"That barn I'm filling now. I started a few months ago, selecting the horses more carefully than I've ever selected in my life." He could hear the sadness in her voice. "I chose them for the veterans."

"Who is that manager?" It wasn't an idle question. He was trying to place all of the people he'd either met or knew about from his research.

"I am. For now." Her voice held an edge.

"Your brother came home from Afghanistan wounded."

Her feet stopped moving, and he saw the slight jerk of her head, as if he'd sent the slenderest of arrows through her. She didn't question his knowledge, of course. She would've expected him to do his homework before coming to see her facilities.

The look she turned on him was filled as much with anger as with anguish. "He was passed from one hospital to another, assigned to one reviewer after another. He couldn't get the quality of help he needed from them and he wouldn't take it from me." She started walking again, seeming not to care if he followed or not.

Camp didn't bother to apologize. There were no words adequate. What was happening in military units everywhere was inexcusable. But there were those working hard to make improvements, and he was part of that effort. No matter how pretty—how beautiful—he found Avery Wilson, he'd verify she was part of the improvement process, as well, or turn her over to the authorities in a heartbeat if he found she was not. Maybe not without a pang, but he'd do it.

The last trace the military had of her brother was that he was one of the walking wounded, lost and homeless, but—hopefully—still alive someplace, still with the possibility of recovery. There was another whole investigative branch now dedicated to finding and helping, this time truly helping, those who would let them. And still, not each of them would.

"What about the young man who was outside the barn last night?"

"Dax?" She shrugged. "He's a stray of sorts. Like Callahan."

Camp had noted the military-issue boots, now he made a mental note to learn his story and, with a soldier, there was no better way than a face to face. He'd already researched Leanne and Tucker and Marla along with Avery Wilson and Eddie Danson. They'd all been in the file handed to him along with this assignment. But not this Dax. Camp would soon remedy that.

Marla intercepted them before they reached Barn Two. Camp noted that she was dressed much like Avery, in jeans and tucked shirt with her light-colored hair pulled up into some kind of knot. Also, like Avery she wore a minimum of makeup. These were women with a focus on their work not their appearance.

She acknowledged Camp with a glance and something that could have passed for a nod but she focused her gaze on Avery. "I've ordered all new headstalls for Barn One.

We're using what we need from Barn Three until they arrive."

"That works," Avery agreed. "You ordered from Barton's?"

"Of course." Marla almost smiled. "I know your preference for local, and the quality is there as well as value for the price. Sam was thrilled to get the order." The smile, that never quite was, disappeared quickly. "There was an odd message on the business line. A Mr. Inghram. He said his flight would arrive a little after one o'clock this afternoon, and he'd be around shortly after to assess the colt."

"What? What colt? Why?"

Camp noted that every bit of the tension was back in Avery's voice.

"I don't know, Avery. That's all he said other than he mentioned an e-mail he'd sent last evening. He sounded like a Yankee or a Brit," Marla added. "I couldn't place the accent."

"I don't care if he sounded like European royalty. He's wasting his time. And mine. We've nothing for sale, lease, or borrow."

"I know," Marla soothed. "I'll deal with him if you like."

"No, it's mine to do, but thank you. I've got this. There is something you can do for me."

"Anything, of course."

"I need a rental vehicle for a few weeks and I need the insurance adjustor to go by the sheriff's office and request to see my SUV so that a claim can get started."

"What are you talking about? Avery, were you in a wreck? Did you get checked by a doctor?" Marla started to sound frantic.

Avery put both hands on Marla's shoulders. "No and no. No wreck and I'm not hurt. Someone had a little fun with my car, that's all. Nothing a new windshield and four new tires won't fix."

* * *

Camp realized she didn't mention bullet holes and a front seat that would need replacing. But since Marla showed clear signs of panic, that was a wise decision on her part.

"Oh, my God, what did he do? He's crazy. I swear it. Avery, I'm sorry."

"Stop, Marla. Stop, okay? I don't know who did it and neither do you. The sheriff may figure it out so let's just wait and see."

"Why are you protecting him?"

"I'm not, Marla, but until I know more, I can't accuse Eddie of anything."

"Well, I can." With the panic fading, Marla's blue eyes held pure anger. "I can and will."

"I wish you wouldn't."

Marla touched Avery's face lightly. "You're a saint, you know that don't you?" But she didn't, Camp noted, give in to Avery's wishes.

Avery stood watching as Marla walked away, but Camp's attention was split between the two women. Avery's brows were drawn together in worry as she watched her stepdaughter's long strides. Marla glanced at Callahan as the gray cat sauntered by, but she didn't slow. Clearly, Marla on a mission could be a formidable person.

"Well, okay, then." The words were quietly spoken.

Camp focused on Avery and raised one brow.

"There's no stopping Marla when she sets her mind on something. She's wrong though. I'm not a saint. If I could give Eddie as much misery as he's given me, I don't have much doubt that I would. Fortunately for me, he's saved me the effort." She turned at the sound of a diesel engine. A sharp, electric-blue truck was pulling to a stop in front of the second of the three barns. "There's our nine o'clock. You can watch Tucker. He's manager for Barn Two. The youngsters adore him."

* * *

From the look Camp Kirkland is giving Avery, he's feeling a bit of adoration himself, well, at least a pointed interest in her as a female. I don't have much use for romance as a side bar to the tangled mess going on around this place. Beyond that, I'm a bit antsy, as the locals might say. Nothing I can touch a paw to but there's something too quiet about the morning after yesterday's antics. I'll stay close at hand in case mischief comes calling. Whoever fired those bullets last evening hasn't obtained the prize. It may be up to me to make sure that remains the case.

For all of the conflict, the ranch isn't a bad place to be. The stout fence rails all around and fat corner posts make for comfortable places to sit and watch. Not large enough to curl up for a nap, but I can find a place for that easy enough.

I watch as a boy steps down from the truck. He moves with an unusual kind of calm. Kids that age are typically more rambunctious. Odd. He looks healthy, but there's a distinct sadness in his father's eyes as he stands back and watches. I'm guessing the man is his father, anyway. They bear a close resemblance. The boy walks toward a small silvery gray horse led by a wiry man with outrageously red hair and kind green eyes. I'm partial to green eyes, lots of cute female cats have them. I'm not, however, partial to children much of the time. I tolerate them, more so the polite ones, but it's a take 'em or leave 'em kind of thing. I'm also not keen on horses although I'll admit some are magnificent. This one is a bit undersized to be called magnificent but I suppose, to a child, it could seem quite large.

I still don't see fear. The boy looks relaxed as he gets near the horse and the person called Tucker. Tucker smiles but the child doesn't, at least not until he settles quietly into the saddle. The smile he gives his father when he feels secure changes his whole face, and the sadness leaves his father's eyes.

Camp stands near Avery as she watches the boy lift the reins. She explains that the little horse is a Connemara pony and Camp leans even closer, as if to hear her better; I suppose that is a handy excuse for him. Autistic, she says about the boy, with signs of improvement. I wince at the word and her explanation.

"Autism is a hard thing for a parent to work through with a child. I know many don't even try or give up when the progress is too little."

"I've heard it's like the child is there, locked deep inside his own private prison," *Camp answers.*

"That's as good an analogy as any. Medical science is finding new ways to break through the barriers for some. Meanwhile we're doing what we can, here, as animals seem to reach them in ways humans can't."

Camp seems impressed. There may be a possibility he'll realize that Avery is more than just a pretty face. That thought takes a backseat when I hear Avery mention lunch. With any luck, there will be a better attempt than the warmed slice of bread that passed for her breakfast this morning. At midday, Dax eats with the bunkhouse crew, which consists of Tucker and the part-time help. Tucker's efforts with pots and pans aren't terrible, but I'm hoping for something more from Avery than what I've seen from him, so far.

Chapter 4

Tension built slowly through Avery as she sliced fresh, heirloom tomatoes and cucumbers still warm from her small side garden. How *had* she come to be in this domestic little scene with Camp Kirkland? She didn't want to be here. She didn't want *him* to be here. She wanted him to figure out what he needed to know and go away, back to wherever he came from and give her application a thumbs-up when he got there. She wanted to spend the next hour or so pacing the floor while she worried about this unknown Mr. Inghram who thought it okay to show up for a look at one of her horses as if he were answering a sales ad. He planned to arrive with nothing more than a brief voice message and an e-mail she still hadn't had a chance to read much less answer. She wanted to be peaceful, damn it. That didn't seem too much to ask.

She shot a frustrated glance through the glass door where Camp was turning fish on the grill. Dax's cat wove through his legs as if they were best friends. Unexpectedly, the humor of the situation, of her own thoughts, struck her and some of the tension ebbed. So, okay, she wasn't ready to feel attraction for any man, wasn't ready for the attraction she felt for *this* particular man. She didn't need to act on it. And Camp seemed unaware of her interest, of the fact that she found the intelligence in his gaze attractive and his lips tempting when they curved in a smile. He had a nice smile, nothing wrong with admitting that. No reason for the silent admission to kick her pulse up to anxiety level. She was being ridiculous.

Taking a deep breath, she finished what she was doing and stepped into her office to find Mr. Inghram's e-mail. She read through it twice but was none the wiser. He wrote as if she should be expecting him, expecting his e-mail, his phone call, his arrival. It was a polite note, but read as if the purchase were a *done deal*. His imminent arrival was beyond her control. The e-mail had been sent, he mentioned, from his iPad as he stood at the boarding gate. Well, he was destined for disappointment. Her horses were not for sale.

The sound of the door opening drew her back into the kitchen. Camp handed her the platter of grilled-to-perfection red snapper she'd pulled from the freeze earlier, and Callahan immediately shifted his twining from Camp's legs to hers.

Camp gave him a stern glare. "Traitor."

"Fickle, is he?"

"His affections appear to follow the food."

Camp smiled, and her pulse gave that tiny leap again. She felt like calling her own body a traitor but that would be far too much of a confession, even if it were a silent one.

"I thought we'd eat here, instead of the dining room." She indicated the wide, quartz topped bar where she'd already laid out flatware on napkins and glasses filled with ice and water. She didn't want him to think she was going to any trouble to impress him. New Hope Ranch should be impressive enough, *was* impressive enough on its own.

While Camp stepped into the downstairs powder room to wash up, she placed the fish and fresh garden vegetables on the bar along with the salt and pepper grinders. And took another deep breath.

* * *

Camp doesn't seem to have botched the job of grilling. I won't say I'm impressed but I'm not disappointed. Yet. I suspect Avery would prefer he pack his briefcase and all those nicely pressed clothes—yeah, I did a little snooping in his quarters—and depart. For myself, I wouldn't mind if he sticks around to man the grill for another meal or two. Dax is good with a grill when we find one but here it's been mostly heated cans of food for us. I wish I could say I don't have my suspicions about Camp's presence at the ranch although I don't sense any physical threat. He could be what he claims, a desk jockey here to verify the ranch is adequate for wounded veteran rehabilitation. We shall see.

* * *

"Where is Marla's mother?"

Camp had asked a few probing questions about Eddie's role at the ranch, seeming to be satisfied when Avery explained that he'd had very little to do with the physical management of the place. Eddie helped out where he could, at least in the early days, but he had his own business, and sometimes provided an ear to listen when she needed to balance some decision. The question about Eddie's first wife caught Avery by surprise, and she sighed, the heavy weight of sorrow pressing on her even after all these years. "She's deceased. It's a sad story. Eddie's had a lot of loss, and I try to be compassionate because I don't know how much of his current breakdown has to do with that."

"Breakdown? You think he's suffering from some kind of emotional incapacity?" Camp raised his brows, and she could almost feel his skepticism.

"Honestly, I don't know all that is going on with him, maybe not even the half of it," she admitted, "but in the end, I had to accept that I couldn't allow him to destroy what my team and I have worked so hard to build, and he refused any suggestion of professional help. I believe that some diseases are a 'disease of choice.' The victim doesn't choose to have the disease but they do choose—or reject—the opportunity for help and for healing. Marla's been a Godsend to me and she's suffered as much, if not more, than Eddie in all this."

She hesitated, feeling a bit of a traitor to expose her stepdaughter's personal heartache. "Marla's twin died horribly when the girls were eleven. They were both students at the riding facility where I gave lessons at the time but they were in different programs. Marla was in an elevated hunter-jumper class, could have been headed for the Olympics. Missy was placed with me in a therapeutic program."

Camp had stayed silent while she talked, swirling his

water glass while watching the motion of liquid and ice thoughtfully, almost as if to give her space. But at her words, he shifted that piercing gaze to hers. "Therapeutic? Had she been in some kind of accident?"

"No, Missy was born with cerebral palsy. The child was absolutely brilliant academically but walking was difficult for her. She *could* walk with leg braces but was much more mobile, more self-sufficient from her wheelchair. The girls were more than close, as I guess most twins are. But Marla … Marla was devoted to her sister, always came to watch her ride, cheering her on for the slightest victory. She was devastated by Missy's death. They all were. *We* all were." The entire academy had shut down on the day of Missy's funeral. She was that well-loved.

Remembering, Avery focused her attention on her plate, knowing her eyes glittered with tears. She didn't want Camp to see and construe them as some kind of weakness. She didn't want him to see anything that might make her look unfit as a business woman strong enough for the responsibilities associated with a wounded veteran program.

"Had she been progressively ill? I know a little about cerebral palsy, not much, but I know it can impact a number of organs."

Avery shook her head. "No, her death was a horrible, horrible accident. The latch on her wheelchair failed and allowed it to roll into the pool. Marla found her when she came in from after-school softball practice. Marla was into every sport imaginable. Their mother had fallen asleep on the sun porch while Missy sketched. That was one of her favorite pastimes with riding the other. She was very artistic though she only had full use of her right arm. The muscles were stiff and atrophied in the other." Avery still had nightmares, waking to images of Missy slowly sinking into the pool, struggling to release the seatbelt intended to keep her safe when her chair was in use, helpless to free herself as the water closed over her head. She couldn't imagine the horrors that Missy's parents and Marla had endured, thinking about Missy's death.

"She wasn't just a student to you. You loved her," Camp said softly.

"Everyone loved Missy. She was an incredible child. Loving, courageous, sunny ... in spite of her disability. It was a complete tragedy. Her mother took her own life less than a year later and Eddie was left to pick up the pieces. Marla told me once it hurt to the core that she didn't just lose her sister and best friend but that she wasn't reason enough for her mother to want to live."

Camp reached over as if to touch her hand but at the last minute didn't, placing it on the table instead. "I think that's a common and very natural feeling among family members of suicides, even more so with children."

"I won't pretend to know what I'd do in similar circumstances but I can't imagine intentionally leaving my child to face my death and grow up without me."

"You said Marla could have been headed for the Olympics." There was a faint question in his voice.

"She lost heart after Missy died—quit riding, quit everything she enjoyed. Some months after her mother's suicide, Eddie came back to the academy. He was desperate to distract Marla from her grief and thought the horses might help. By then, I'd made the barest beginnings with New Hope Ranch, and he chose to bring her here, thinking it would be an easier environment."

She fell silent for a moment, thinking back to that long ago summer. Camp's steady gaze reminded her of the reason she was sharing all of these personal, sometimes happy, sometimes painful experiences.

"Marla didn't want lessons, not in any of the venues, she wanted only to be around horses and ride on her own. So that's what we did. Mostly long trail rides, just the two of us." It was through those months that she and Eddie had drifted into a relationship. She pushed aside those memories, now tarnished by the ugliness of more recent history.

Avery watched as Camp processed what she'd told him, and she wasn't in the least surprised when he circled back to his initial question and asked, "Do you really think—this many years later—that Eddie suddenly finds it impossible to deal with the losses of his daughter and his wife?"

"No," she admitted. "No, I don't. What I really think is that I missed a weakness in Eddie, missed it at the start and failed to watch it grow. I was too caught up in creating my dreams for this place, too caught up with the hard work and my love for the horses to see what was happening to my husband. And to my marriage."

"What do you think has been happening?"

Avery hesitated. She didn't want to cause herself any additional complications with this man, or rather with the position he held and his assignment here. Still, honesty was all she had to offer. "I've thought at times some kind of addiction … alcohol, maybe even drugs."

"Neither of which would be your fault. Your problem, maybe, but not your *fault*."

The intensity in his voice surprised her until she realized he'd mistaken her meaning. "I agree, it isn't, but I should at least have recognized sooner that it existed. I might have made different decisions." She sighed, realizing she might as well acknowledge an aspect she'd neatly skimmed over in earlier conversation. "Marla manages accounts payables. For a while Eddie managed accounts receivables. I've taken that part of the business on for the time being. I suspect, now, that Eddie was putting a good bit in his pocket right from the first, but a few years ago, the revenue from the ranch started shrinking noticeably. I brought in an independent financial guru to help me maximize my profit. She's the one who found that Eddie was pocketing nearly as much as he was depositing. I confronted him with the proof, he denied it, and I filed for divorce."

None of it had been as easy as that admission must sound to an outsider, but that pain, that drama—and the residual humiliation—was over and done and not anything she wanted, or needed, to relive by talking about it now.

Her cell phone broke the complete silence that followed her stark words. She glanced at the caller I.D., noting the time, and sighed. She looked at Camp before she hit answer. "I guess it's show time." Careful to lighten her tone, she spoke into the phone. "Hey, Tucker."

"There's a Mr. Inghram to see you. He's pulling an empty horse trailer." Tucker sounded worried, and she realized immediately that she should've given her team a heads-up.

"And he'll be pulling an empty one on his way out," she said reassuringly, keeping her voice calm. "Where did he park?"

"In the main drive."

"Tell him I'm on my way. You can go back to your barn. You have a student, don't you?"

"Pulling in now, but I feel like I should be here with you."

She heard the edge in Tucker's voice and knew at once he didn't like the appearance of their *guest*. "I've got this,

Tucker, I promise. Go take care of your student." Her years-long fight with Eddie had affected more than herself. Her team had become protective of her. Too protective.

As she put the phone down, she realized Camp had already gotten to his feet. "Not you, too." She fought the urge to roll her eyes. "I've *got* this," she said, repeating the words she'd spoken to Tucker in exasperation.

"Let's go," was all Camp said.

Irritation washed through her and she flashed Callahan a scowl as he sauntered out of the office and through the door with them. Another alpha male. She was surrounded by them.

* * *

As usual, however, things aren't what they seem. I've got a nose for weaponry, honed since hooking up with Dax, and noted some heavy firepower hidden around Camp's lodging in my snooping earlier. That doesn't add up with what he claims to be his purpose here. Not for me, anyway. My suspicion is that Camp hasn't been a desk jockey for any length of time—if he is at all. His military credentials are real but I'd bet a prime rib he's seen significant military action in the not-too-distant past. Maybe he's what he says. Maybe he's not. I'll dig more when the opportunity pops up. Good thing I was keeping an ear tuned to the kitchen conversation and an eye on the clock. I wouldn't want to miss the excitement.

We head toward the barn area, and I'm not sure why such a rushed pace has been set by the humans. None of us need an all-out hike in this southern sauna of heat and humidity. We can handle what needs handling when we get there.

The first thing that catches my eye is the fancy rig, flashy and shiny with too much chrome, parked directly in the middle of the drive. Either truck or trailer alone cost a mint. They sure don't downgrade the appearance of the main drag into the ranch where someone has spent a small fortune, in money or hours, landscaping and maintaining. The rustic board fence is neat without being over the top. Most places I've seen while rambling with Dax have had white board railing, the farm favorite for years, but a little boring after a time.

I edge closer to the semi and trailer while these humans exchange pleasant comments, none of them mean. I check for the state of registration on the license plate, but find instead TAG APPLIED FOR. As in 'just purchased.' I guess a hired rig wasn't good enough for Mr. Inghram.

Whoa … voices are rising. I leave off investigating to move closer to my humans in case I need to enter the fray.

"What do you mean your horses are not for sale?" *The dude speaking isn't impressive. With thin brows drawn together over a thinner nose and lips pressed together, he looks like an irritable insect. I don't understand the recent wave of shaved heads in human males. Every creature looks better with a healthy covering of hair, or fur, as the case may be.*

"My horses are not for sale. It's that simple." *Avery is keeping calm so far but that silky tone is menacing. I'm impressed. I wouldn't have thought she had it in her.* "I can't imagine why you'd travel from Canada without asking first."

"I'm done talking with you. Where is your husband?"

Whoops, that comment is guaranteed to be insulting to a self-made woman.

"I don't have a husband."

Good comeback. She's being deliberately obtuse with her response. That appeals to me. Maybe not her wisest course but it's fun for an interested bystander. What I don't like is the way Inghram is tapping that crop against his shiny boots.

"Impossible. Of course, you have a husband."

"Why do you think that?" *I see suspicion rising in her eyes.*

She's a smart one.

"Because it was your husband who took money for the animal. Half last month and half to be paid today. Cash."

The figure he names is high if the widening of Avery's eyes is any indication.

"I'm truly sorry for you, Mr. Inghram. You've been cheated but not by me. I've taken money from no one because—as I said—my horses are not for sale. Not now, not ever."

What an idiot. And a potential threat as well. He steps closer, puffing out his chest. Well, as best he can, there's not much of it there, and I'll bet it's also hairless. Camp is moving in as well, and he has no need for any pathetic effort to appear bigger or stronger than he is. "I believe you're done here."

Mr. Inghram must see he's outmanned. He steps back but not down. "Not until I've loaded Mr. Tarent's animal."

For some reason, the name Tarent lights a match to a tinderbox. Avery's hands are shaking now and not in fear.

"Tarent? Neal Tarent? That despicable man will never own one of my horses. He may be rich enough to buy from some, but not from me. His mishandling has destroyed some of the finest animals in the world."

"Ridiculous! Mr. Tarent is highly respected in his field. He's obtained, and I have trained, dozens of horses to success in the show ring." *This guy is offended, but I don't have any sympathy for him. He needs to close his trap and move on while he can.*

"The ones you didn't manage to cripple, you mean." *There's fire in her eyes now. She's the one stepping forward, ready to do battle—physical, I suspect, more than mental. That could prove a good show, but I won't let it get out of hand.* "Get off my property. Now. Before I call the sheriff."

"Oh, I can promise you the law will most certainly get involved. Your husband implied you might be obstinate, but Mr. Tarent's influence is wide, and he's spent a fortune on this transaction. This truck and trailer were delivered from Tennessee this week, awaiting my arrival at the airport. I assure you, he didn't purchase those, as well as pay an astronomical amount for a yearling of the famous Flying Jackanapes, to lose both the animal and the money."

"Jack and his offspring are not for sale and, if they were, it would never be to the likes of either you or Mr. Tarent. I don't care how influential you feel yourself to be. Neither of you have any power or control over me. People like the two of you were responsible for Jack nearly being destroyed when he was put back in the ring barely healed from surgery to remove a bone spur. He tore a tendon performing his heart out for his owners, and they would have put him down for his loyalty! I rescued him just in time and his babies will never be for sale."

"Your husband took Mr. Tarent's currency. There will be consequences."

"Take it up with my ex! If he fleeced you, your problem is with him, not with me. I've taken no one's money and mine is the sole name on the papers of any horse on this property and the only name that ever has been. Now get out. Go."

Well, well, well, it looks like this confrontation is about to get physical. Camp is done with the exchange and closing in for the kill. "Mr. Inghram, I suggest your employer focus his attention on the person who swindled him. You have about five minutes to back this flashy rig out of here. After that you'll be held here until the law arrives and charges you with trespassing."

Mr. Inghram is either a complete fool or has a desire for assisted suicide. He thrusts his chin and glares at Camp with contempt. He'd better chose his words carefully or a fist fight will be next up!

"Her husband said she was slutting with the hired help. I guess you'd be one of them." *This guy has overplayed his hand. Even Avery is shocked.*

"Four minutes." *Camp seems to be a man of great restraint, but if the fists clenched at his side are any sign, I'd say he'd be happy to use force instead of words.*

I'd rather the countdown not drag on. The heat is suffocating, and I'd rather be under a shady tree.

Good! The man has at least some sense of self-preservation. He takes one step backward and then pivots. His flanks are as narrow as the rest of him. Not badly clothed, but very narrow.

* * *

Camp watched as Avery stood with clenched hands until Inghram climbed back into the semi and backed it with more caution than skill down the long drive. Avery could have stepped to one side and allowed the man to make the full circle. The drive had been designed to offer large trailers an easy turn. He hoped Avery's pointed action wasn't lost on the bastard.

The tears in her eyes when she turned struck him in the gut. That they were tears of fury, rather than of sorrow, made them no less wrenching.

"I'm going to *kill* him."

She wasn't, Camp knew, referring to either Inghram or Tarent.

Chapter 5

As Inghram cautiously exited her property, Avery turned to find Leanne and Tucker at her heels. Both looked as furious as she felt.

"Jerk," Leanne muttered.

Tucker snorted, his glare fixed on the shiny truck and trailer. "Jackass, I'd say."

"You heard his claim?" Avery asked.

"Enough." Leanne's angry glance turned to worry. "You think he's telling the truth?"

Avery sighed. "I do, which means we need to keep a close watch on things for a while. Eddie's going to be frantic if he's taken that much of a man's cash for an animal he doesn't own and can't produce. Inghram said yearling, but I've no doubt all of the horses are at risk. And for who knows how long."

"I'll put a cot by the yearling paddock tonight," Tucker said grimly.

Leanne nodded agreement. "And I'll sleep in my barn. Close to Jack. And maybe we should keep Jack and his working offspring in their stalls at night for now so we can watch them. We'll have to get them out for a few hours during the day between their appointment times."

That would be extra work for her team, and Avery absolutely hated the thought of not giving all of the animals every hour of their precious paddock time. The yearlings had a long open-sided shed for shelter in their pasture, but unless there were storms in the forecast, the others were up during the intense heat of the day and turned out at night when temperatures were milder and the sun wasn't a blistering orb overhead. Still, she couldn't disagree with Leanne's rationale. The safety of the horses was paramount.

As much as she wanted to tell her team these precautions wouldn't be necessary, she feared they might be. "It seems Eddie really had expected a different ruling from the judge," she admitted as much to herself as to her team.

As Leanne and Tucker went back to their barns and their work for the afternoon, she felt Camp's patient gaze on her and turned back to him with a sigh. None of this would look good in regard to her application. It was hard not to feel discouraged when she should have been able to enjoy the euphoria of her divorce being finalized and the ranch still safely in her name. Eddie had no legal claim to land or horses, but it seemed he didn't plan to let that stop him.

Camp didn't say anything for a minute, then he asked, "How much of an alarm system do you have?"

She blinked, pulling her mind in this new direction. "Well, it's pretty good for foaling mares but I doubt it would be much use for preventing theft. I've got cameras set up in the box stalls. I guess we could shift those toward the main entrance to the barn and figure out how to better secure the side exits. It might take some rewiring." Avery felt completely out of her element at the thought. "I might be able to get the guy who installed them to come out and make the adjustments."

"Let me study the setup first. It may be a matter of repositioning the cameras without moving them all that far."

Avery hesitated, looking into his eyes and trying to gauge his thoughts around what was happening at the ranch and her future plans. "You don't have to help me do this, you know? I don't want to delay what you're here to do. Getting approved by your government for the veteran equine therapy program is important to me."

Camp raised his brow quizzically. "*My* government?"

She winced at her own word choice. "I'm not much into the political scene but sometimes I think those of us who have to work to survive have been abandoned by the politicians."

Camp's smile was slow and sexy. Not something she wanted to think about right now for sure.

"Let's put that conversation on hold for another time. I've read through ample files for now, and I've got plenty to absorb. Sometimes keeping my hands busy while I think things through allows me to keep those thoughts productive."

"Okay." She hesitated. "Is there anything I can do to help?"

"Be on standby in case I need something from a building supply store."

"Actually, I've got some errands to run in town." It was a spur of the moment decision, but he didn't need to know that. "If you find you need something, Tucker can call me."

"I've got a better idea." He pulled his phone from his pocket. "What's your number? That way I won't have to disturb Tucker if he's giving a lesson."

She hesitated a moment before giving it to him, then realized he had ways to access it if he wanted to do that. A moment later a soft ding sounded in the silence between them.

He looked at her. "Now you have mine as well."

The moment felt uncomfortably intimate, as if they weren't standing in the middle of her drive in the afternoon heat talking about ranch security.

"Do you need to take my truck?" It was a reminder that her vehicle was incapacitated—and why.

"No, there's a work truck. It's not pretty, but it runs well. Marla uses it more than any of us, when the ranch needs something that isn't big enough to schedule a full delivery."

"You'll be back before dark?" His tone was too casual, and he smiled at the scowl she shot him and lifted his hands in a gesture of innocence. "Hey, in case I need you to bring back something to ensure security here is as effective as we can make it."

Although she still suspected his goal was to make sure she was at the ranch before nightfall, she didn't argue the point. There was peril out there. She couldn't even begin to guess the next direction Eddie would take. In fact, if Marla wasn't back when she returned, she'd check on her as well. Touching base for safety's sake was something they'd not felt necessary in the past but it certainly seemed warranted now.

* * *

It's a dilemma. Do I stay here and secure the perimeters? Do I dog the heels of my temporary human? Now there's an apt turn of phrase. Dog the heels. Canines are insecure and submissive creatures, always at their masters' beck and call. Cats don't submit, and we don't have masters. We have humans we choose as companions. Dax and I chose each other. This ranch is where we have elected to be, at least for now. In return for decent food and a comfortable place to sleep, we owe some allegiance to the woman who owns it.

So there. That's my answer. As valuable as the ranch is to its owner, more prized is the owner to the people who depend on her. Her protection comes first, and I feel a sense of duty to accompany and safeguard Avery Wilson.

Now my difficulty will be to either convince her that it's best I'm at her side or to make sure I'm detected too late for her to stop my accompanying her. Since she doesn't know me well enough to appreciate my abilities, I decide to take the less obvious route. While she gathers whatever she needs from inside, I'll scout around to locate and investigate this work truck and hope that it's both accessible and more comfortable than that description sounds.

I find what I think is the vehicle in question behind what the humans refer to as Barn One. It's more than a little dusty but not nasty, has a scratch or a dozen in the bed which I've accessed with a quick leap. There sure doesn't look to be much in the way of comfort or camouflage back here. Hmmm, luck is with me. A front window is lowered and there's enough footing for me to walk along the top of the doors and climb through. And, more luck, although the floorboard isn't carpeted, I think that's what's called a stadium throw on the back seat. A little tug and—there—it's now on the floor and I'm out of obvious sight. In fact, if I nudge my way in a bit more, I'm almost positive I'm not visible at all, even should Avery wisely peer into the back before climbing in herself.

The door opens, and there she is. Sure enough, she leans over for a quick peek before settling into the front. If I judged the distance from town accurately, I should have time for a small nap on my return there.

* * *

Avery loved the town she'd chosen as her own. There was a quaintness that spoke to that sentimental part of her but also a bustling energy that promised growth and success for the future. Her future. Despite the continued threat of Eddie's antics, she felt hopeful now for the first time in a long time. The weight of that failed marriage was lifted.

Parking in front of the sheriff's office, she stepped out and was somehow not surprised to see Callahan's gray pelt emerge from the back seat before she could close the door of the truck. "Really?" she asked in exasperation.

He flicked his scarred ear in her direction. Two brilliant golden orbs blinked, unfazed by her less than welcoming expression. Rolling her own eyes, Avery picked him up and carried him inside with her.

Sheriff Farley was waiting in his office as he'd promised to be when she'd called on her drive into town. He lifted his brows at the cat in her arms but didn't comment as he stood and stepped around his desk to give her a quick hug. He closed the door to the open area where the dispatcher and a small scattering of officers were dealing with the mountains of paperwork associated with law enforcement. Despite the busy atmosphere, the place had a sense of order to the chaos. Paper everywhere; dust nowhere. That was Ben's influence, she knew. He came across as a rough and tumble sort of man, but she'd never seen him in a uniform that was rumpled or stained unless the damage had occurred in the line of duty.

Before Eddie came along, Ben had asked her out to dinner while picking up his emotional pieces after a tumultuous divorce. She'd agreed on condition they went as friends, sharing the check along with dinner, conversation, and a bottle of wine. That friendship had worked for them better than any romance could have and stood strong to this day. Ben had since re-married very happily.

With the door closed, Avery placed Callahan on the floor. She wasn't sure why she was taking so much care to keep him close and safe. This had to be one cat that was completely self-sufficient. Maybe it was because he seemed to be keeping an eye on her as well.

"Sit down, Avery." There was real concern in the southern inflection of Ben's gravelly voice. He waited until she did, then took the chair beside hers, on the visitor side of his desk. "How are you?"

"Frustrated," she said honestly. "I should be happy and peaceful and I'm frustrated that I'm not—that I can't be. I knew Eddie would be angry, even hostile, at the judge's decision but now it seems he's way more than that. I think he's a very, very desperate man." She described the scene with Inghram, concluding, "…and that's on top of the damage to my SUV. I mean, honestly, Ben, bullets?"

The concern in his eyes deepened. "Those bullets came from a high-powered rifle some distance away. That wasn't someone who whipped a concealed carry out of his pocket and fired in a moment of anger. It was planned and accurate, assuming the windshield was the intended target."

"So, it could have been an accident. Someone shooting at something or someone else and my SUV was in the way."

"Could have been."

She read his tone. "But you don't think so."

She glanced down as the cat hissed softly. Callahan didn't think so either if the restless whipping of his tail was any indication. He aimed his stare on the sheriff's face.

"No, I don't, not unless they were shooting at Eddie while he was hell-bent on cutting your tires," he admitted, "and I think that's a real possibility. In any case, I suggest you keep your guard up every second."

Her shoulders sagged. "I will, Ben, but this isn't what I need to be doing. I need to get busy repairing the financial damage Eddie's already done to the ranch, not worrying about what additional mischief he's planning."

Ben rubbed his clean-shaven jaw. "Avery, I'll tell you, I'm not so sure the damage to your SUV was Eddie's doing, at least not from an intentional standpoint. From what I've been hearing, I'd say Eddie's gotten himself in pretty deep debt, maybe with some pretty nasty people."

"Just what is it you're hearing?" Avery heard the trepidation in her own voice. "What kind of nasty people?"

"High-flyers … big league gamblers. You knew Eddie frequented the casinos quite a bit?"

Avery nodded. It was no secret around town, either, she knew. Frustratingly, she'd had to pay Eddie's delinquent accounts with more than one local tradesperson until her attorney had secured a legal separation in advance of the actual divorce. That document had allowed him to post in the paper on her behalf stating she was no longer financially responsible for Eddie's debts.

"Well, seems he's been playing with money that wasn't his to spend, trading on what he hoped to get from the divorce settlement. That fancy trainer at your place this morning? His employer called me about five minutes after you did. Wanted a deputy to escort the rig back out to the ranch to *claim his property*. Somehow thought I'd be impressed with his credentials. He's got a better grasp of the situation now, and I hope he's too smart to do anything illegal, but we can't count on that. And there's no telling who else is out there that Eddie's made some kind of deal with. Eddie's in over his head, Avery, and he's made some very bad characters very angry."

Panic hit Avery deep in her gut. "What are you saying? I need to worry about real danger, someone doing physical harm, to the ranch, to Leanne and Tucker as well as Marla and the horses?"

"I'm afraid that's exactly what I'm saying. You've got my personal cell. Don't hesitate, not even one minute, to use it if something doesn't seem right, feel right, smell right. You *call* me." His words were emphatic.

Avery felt sick to her stomach as she stood to leave the office. "When can I have my SUV back?"

"As soon as it's repaired. We've found all we're going to there. I called the dealership, and they picked it up with orders to replace the tires and windshield and front seat. They're to have it detailed inside and out. I let your insurance agent take some photos while it was here and everything's approved, said she'd get the paperwork out to you in a day or two. They'll call you when it's ready."

"Oh, Ben," her voice caught, "that's above and beyond. I appreciate it so much."

"And I'm not done with this investigation, Avery, I promise. Now you let me know at once if anything suspicious happens. No hesitation. No matter how small it seems to you."

Ben hugged her again on her way out, a friendly, reassuring hug that did nothing to reassure her. Nothing at all.

* * *

And wasn't that good news? Ha! But nothing I didn't expect. I had Eddie Danson pegged for a scoundrel from the moment I spied him threatening Avery. I tend to agree with the sheriff's evaluation of things, as little as I like it. There is evil on every corner. Avery's woes were in no way resolved with the thud of a gavel and the granting of a divorce.

Somehow, I have to make sure she shares what she's learned with Camp. He has resources that can complement my natural abilities.

* * *

Out on the sidewalk, Avery checked her phone. Nothing yet from Camp. She hesitated, tempted to check with the dealership, though it seemed unlikely they could have her SUV ready that afternoon. Besides, there were things she needed to pick up at the feed store as well as from the hardware that were better suited to the work truck. She could have everything delivered, of course, but her nerves were jangling, and she needed the normalcy of running errands, of taking care of business. Her business.

She was greeted warmly at the feed store and felt completely comfortable putting Callahan down to roam on the wide-planked wood flooring. The earthy scent of feed, stored hay, and gardening supplies helped settle her nerves.

"What are you needing today, Ms. Avery?" The clerk was summer college help for Barton Feed, but Avery had always known her to represent the interests of the owner well. Kim was casual in denim but her tee was neatly tucked into the waist of those jeans. Avery envied her the easy, breezy attitude of youth but not the remembered burden of working her own way through an education.

"I don't need much," Avery admitted. "Marla will be placing the regular order tomorrow, I think. I mostly wanted to stop in and see what you have new by way of tack. I for sure need to pick up a couple of wheelbarrows. I've got the truck so we can load them in the back."

"I heard about your car," Kim said sympathetically. Her glance was curious, but she didn't press when Avery simply nodded in response. "What style of wheelbarrow did you want?"

"The oversized hard plastic we got last time worked out well. It hasn't rusted out like the metal ones always do. I'm tired of us having to share between the barns and I'm hoping I have Barn Three full and in business before the end of the year."

"Well, you're in luck. We've got some in stock, right now." While Kim picked up a radio from the counter and spoke to someone in the yard, Avery crossed over to the wall of tack bright with rhinestones. "I need you to load two of those heavy-duty wheelbarrows into Ms. Danson's truck. Yes, the black ones." She listened again to the other side of the exchange. "Thanks."

"What else can I get for you today, Ms. Avery? Something with glitter and shine?" Kim's tone was hopeful though she'd know from experience that wasn't the style typically delivered to the ranch. Marla held to the durable, good quality leather equipment the store kept on hand or special ordered for the ranch.

"Not for me, but sometimes I think something sparkly would be real pretty on Jack."

"Maybe for his Christmas present this year," Kim joked.

"Could be," Avery gave her quick smile, "but that's all for today. I need to get back and I still have to hit the hardware store. And, for the record, I've taken my maiden name, Wilson, back as part of the divorce proceedings."

As Kim readied her ticket for signature, Avery looked around for Callahan. He sat near the door, watching the opening, for all the world like a guard dog. The thought amused her but then she recalled that she might well need a guard dog before this was done—for the horses though—not for herself.

Kim handed her the ticket and said, "I got an e-mail today. Our new calendars should be in this week."

Avery was surprised. "Do they always come in this early?"

"The first order, yes. We always end up making several re-orders and I expect we'll sell even more this year. I think when everyone sees the beautiful photographs of the horses of New Hope Ranch along with the lovely pond scenes from the McPherson place, these will go quick."

Avery smiled. "I love that old McPherson Pond, and the horses were cooperative with the photographer, though Marla had to do some real clowning around to get both Jack's ears forward at the same time."

Kim chuckled. "Well, you and Marla sure rivaled the horses!"

"That's sweet of you to say, Kim, thank you. Be sure to call me when they come in. We'll buy several dozen to give as gifts to our clients. Good advertising, you know."

Advertising she didn't actually need. The ranch was already growing *almost* faster than she could keep up. Still, she felt good about helping the local merchants which was why she'd agreed to have the ranch featured. Neither she nor Marla had been keen on being in any of the shots, and they'd done their best to keep the focus on the horses who were the real stars as far as they were concerned.

"Come on, Callahan," she said when she reached the door. "We've got another stop to make. Maybe by then, Mr. Kirkland will have let me know what he needs for the camera system."

As careful as she was to call him Mr. Kirkland, even to the cat, Avery knew she'd already begun to think of Camp in much more familiar terms. She even liked the sound of his name in her mind.

Chapter 6

Camp stepped down from the ladder and contemplated his progress. Angling one camera toward the barn's main entrance was helpful but there wasn't adequate wiring to allow him to move the other cameras to more strategic locations. He measured the distance by the simple method of walking the route and calculating feet per stride. It was crude but effective. He added that total to the text message he'd begun along with some necessary connectors, not yet hitting send as he hadn't scoped out requirements in the two remaining barns.

His handy sixth sense warned him he wasn't alone in the barn, but there wasn't a corresponding tingle along the back of his neck. He made no move toward his concealed carry as he stepped around the corner.

Tucker, tall and lanky, was squinting up at the camera Camp had shifted. "Good idea, that. You planning on moving the others?"

"Yeah, but I'll have to wait until Ms. Wilson returns from town. I want to move a couple to the other barns."

Tucker frowned. "Avery went by herself?"

Camp studied him, trying to judge his age. Early thirties, maybe mature twenties. "She did. That worry you?"

"Shouldn't it? That son of a bitch she married shot her windshield out, didn't he? Who knows what he'll aim at next. Or what other badass he's pissed off."

"We don't know for sure whose bullets those were … unless you've heard from the sheriff." Camp doubted any solid proof would connect the vandalism to Eddie Danson. He wasn't even convinced that Eddie's finger had been on the trigger, at least not the physical trigger of the gun. Eddie had maybe incited the incident, as he'd precipitated Inghram's ill-fated trip to the ranch earlier. Camp didn't credit him with being macho enough to put a bullet into her vehicle in the middle of town.

"Marla told me it had to be her dad. She should know." Tucker sounded slightly defensive, and Camp took a closer look at the younger man. He recognized a gleam in Tucker's eyes that was at least infatuation, and maybe even some stronger emotion.

"Likely she should and perhaps does, but it's always a better bet not to assume anything when a threat of danger is involved. If you guard in a single direction—because you think you know—you leave yourself wide open on several other fronts."

Tucker hunched his narrow shoulders. "Avery said you were military."

Camp smiled inwardly. As if the word military

explained everything about him to the young man. After nearly three decades of active service, Camp had accepted a desk job. He considered it a weak moment when he'd been recovering from a second injury with the first barely healed. At the time it had seemed ideal, no one shooting at him, no one's life depending upon him, traveling around the many states that he had loved and served and sacrificed a pint or two of blood to protect. All he had to do was review, visit, and certify therapeutic complexes, equestrian and otherwise, across the country as government-approved to offer services to veterans whose wounds crossed the gamut from loss of sight and limb to brain trauma and PTSD.

Even so, if his first case on the job involved bringing to ruin the most attractive woman he'd seen in all his travel across the globe, he'd be looking to pick up a gun again. New Hope Ranch had been approved by his predecessor who hadn't been considered a singular success in his role. Camp wondered if Avery Wilson was one of the man's failures. Someone was guilty of fraud. One possibility was Eddie Danson, the other was Avery. Her team, Tucker among them, wouldn't agree with that possibility but Camp couldn't afford to ignore it.

Like most people, Tucker didn't have a clue what the term *military* conveyed, including the search for truth, whatever the cost. Camp hoped he never did, never had to, but all he said was, "Yes, I am. Are you busy right now? Do you have time to check out the other barns? I could use your help."

Tucker straightened, clearly pleased to be asked. "Yeah, I've had my last client for the day. I've got a couple hours before I need to do anything else with my horses."

My horses. Camp liked hearing that sense of ownership, that tone of affection. It boded well for the success of Avery Wilson's venture. And then he wondered why he cared. The fact that he did bothered him. A lot. Neutrality was crucial in searching for answers and reaching the truth.

After walking through the remaining two barns with Tucker and stepping off some additional measurements, Camp added to his text message to Avery, hit send and then found himself waiting for her response. Tucker had taken himself off to collect some boards and nails and tools to build temporary bases for the cameras Camp planned to move. Camp found himself glad the younger man wasn't there to see him staring at his phone like some teen waiting for a response. Decisively, he slipped the phone into his pocket. He had no idea how often Avery Wilson checked her messages or if she kept the volume down to minimize distractions. He was, however, certain she'd check before she headed out of town to see if he needed anything to help keep her horses safe. No bones about it, they were her priority.

Tucker returned, pulling a utility cart stacked with boards and tools, and they worked companionably for a little while. Camp wasn't surprised to find Tucker less than talkative but it was an easy silence broken only by necessity for the work involved. Leanne stopped by after her last client of the day to see if they needed help but didn't seem disappointed to be told they were good. Tucker asked her to make a round of the barns and paddocks.

"Sure thing," Leanne agreed easily. "Then I'll see if I can unearth some of the cots and blankets we use for kids' camp. I need to go home to check in with Jason, but I'm coming back here for the night. Hopefully all of this will settle down soon." She grinned. "I haven't seen the appeal in sleeping under the stars or in a barn since I was twelve or so."

"Kids' camp?" Camp asked into the quiet that followed her departure.

"Yep. Avery started it her first year. I think it was mostly to help Marla. She was little more than a kid then, and it was soon after her mother's suicide. I wasn't here for the first camp, but I was for the second and I've helped with all of them since then."

"This was the first place you ever worked?"

"First and only. I was a kid when I started here, every day after school. I traded cleaning stalls for lessons because my folks didn't earn enough for things like that."

"I noticed some of the help mucking stalls and scrubbing water tubs seem young. They're high school?"

Tucker nodded. "Mostly. We've got a junior and a senior and one college freshman."

Camp mentally dropped those three to lower on his list of possible suspects—not off, but lower.

"Once I hit college, I added weekends and evenings to pay for tuition and books and as many meals as I could afford. I knew from the start Avery would make a success of this place. When I got my degree, she hired me straight on."

"Yeah?" Camp paused before he hammered the next nail. "What's your degree?"

"Veterinary medicine." There was enormous pride evident in the answer.

Camp lowered his hammer and scrutinized more closely the young man he'd recognized as intelligent but hadn't given nearly enough attention to as someone with drive and ambition. He was also struck by the realization that New Hope Ranch had the resources to afford an on-staff veterinarian.

Tucker grinned. "I know. I look like a kid. I hear that all the time. It helps out with some of my younger clients who open up to me more than they might have."

"Do you have a practice? Away from here, I mean?" Camp was more than curious about the arrangement.

"Nope. Could have I guess, but Avery pays me well. Raises are small but regular and I know business here is only going to get bigger and better. Right now, I stay busy and earn my salary giving lessons along with the foaling and taking care of routine vaccinations and minor injuries here and there. I do help out some of the neighboring farms if the vet in town is tied up with an emergency but I don't charge them for it. That's part of being good neighbors in a close community. As a matter of fact, I plan to make some rounds this evening after the horses are fed and settled. I want to ask a few of those I've helped to keep an eye open for strangers wandering around."

Camp resumed work and put the last nail in place. "Sounds like you've got a good future mapped out right here."

"That's the plan." Tucker stepped back from the ladder as Camp descended. "Once these barns are full and Barns Four and Five are built and filled with horses, Avery's going to build a real clinic. We'll need it by then. She's drawn up the design already, has an apartment for me up top." He spoke quietly, without any conceit, though Camp suspected not many vets his age had a practice that included housing along with salary.

Camp nodded. "This is going to be quite a place, I

think." It was already.

"So, you're going to approve us for the veteran's program?"

It was like a punch to the gut, being reminded that he had no reason yet to trust Avery Wilson. "I haven't come across any reason not to," he said cautiously. But the truth was, his reason for being there had somehow gotten diverted by the events that had transpired in the last twenty-four hours. And by a pair of green and gold eyes. He'd need to conclude his investigation soon and determine if criminality, negligence, or something else was behind bills received and payments sent by the managing office on behalf of veterans who'd never received any of the benefits of the program here at the ranch.

Camp was glad when a quiet ping from his phone gave him a reason to redirect the conversation. "Ms. Wilson has purchased the fiber optic cable I need for the last runs. She's headed back to the ranch."

Tucker started gathering up tools. "I'll be back later this evening and can give you a hand with running that wire. Lighting's plenty good in the barn for just about anything we need to do."

Camp nodded. "Sure thing." In the meantime, he needed to get back on track with determining the guilt or innocence of one Avery Wilson.

* * *

Even with the lengthy days of summer—which Avery often wished were switched about so that winter and not summer had the extension of daylight—she needed her headlights by the time she turned onto the ranch drive.

Her first thought was one of relief to see Marla's vehicle parked in its usual place. Her second was an unwelcome leap of her pulse as Camp pushed away from the paddock post where he'd been leaning. She watched as his long stride carried him toward the ranch truck. He reached her before she had time to do more than open the driver side door and step out. He'd been waiting and watching for her, that much was clear.

"I see Marla's home." The inane comment seemed better than staring silently into those dark eyes that regarded her with startling intensity. "Is she okay?"

She found the slight quirk of his lips unexpectedly appealing.

"Hard for me to tell. She's either not one for conversation or she doesn't have much she wants to say to me."

Avery went for what she hoped was a casual smile. "Don't take it personally. She's an excellent conversationalist but not much of a talker, if that makes sense." The smile faded. "And all of this has been more than a little hard on her."

"She's a real athlete, though. She's put two horses through their paces since she got back. They were a bit unruly but she handled them expertly."

"Uh-oh—she doesn't paddock ride much—and it's most often when she needs to work off steam. I'd guess she's not happy with the outcome of her talk with Eddie."

"Not much chance that was going to go well, anyway, I'd think." Camp stepped back slightly, and Avery realized how close he'd been standing to her in the shadows beyond the paddock lights. And how right it had felt that he be that close.

She cleared her throat but her voice still sounded a bit husky to her own ears when she told him, "I found everything you thought you'd need."

"Good. Let's get the truck unloaded, shall we?"

* * *

With any luck, Camp made real progress in safeguarding things here while we were in town. I'll make it a point to inspect his handiwork, but I don't have a lot of doubt it will be done, and done well. Whatever his stated purpose—or his true but more subversive one—in being here, I sense the man would throw his life on the line to protect and serve. Failure is not an option, and all that. He'd probably consider any harm to this facility while he's present a failure of monumental proportions.

As the humans have their exchange of the mundane details … cable produced, examined, and pronounced just right … blah, blah, blah … I'm going to have a look around. At some point, these two may realize, accept, and even act upon their mutual physical attraction. It's also possible they will not. In any case, I doubt it will be soon. In either case, I don't have the time or inclination to witness the outcome except as it pertains to the resolution of the threats facing Avery.

At a glance, this isn't the most complex mystery that's caught my interest. Strong female weds inferior male whose true colors come to light over the course of time. Strong female discards and divorces. Inferior male attempts to take by stealth or force what he has not earned. And yet, because I don't consider myself infallible, I'll be honest enough to admit, I think there could be something I'm missing in all of this. To use a hackneyed, but still valid, maxim, I'm convinced that things aren't entirely as they seem.

Should Camp be digging deeper into the tragic deaths of Mr.

Danson's daughter and wife? Accidental drowning? Suicide? Maybe. But maybe not, two deaths in quick succession do seem too much of a coincidence. Was there motive for murder in either and is the remaining daughter now at risk? Maybe I need to keep an eye out for her safety as well. For now, I'll patrol the perimeter of the house, barns, and paddocks, the better to sniff out any human predator. Though what I've heard Dax call heat lightning flickers in the distance, I don't think I'll be at great risk of a drenching. After that, however, a wise and crafty cat needs adequate shut-eye for cognitive thinking.

Hmmm, now there's an oddity, one of the young equines is snorting at the water trough. He seems to want to drink but then backs away with ears pinned. An easy leap has me on the ledge that surrounds it where I'm able to make a closer observation. Uh-oh. That's not good. A dead bird floating and not a small one. I wouldn't want to drink that nastiness either. And enough of an oddity to make me want to look further. Each paddock and each pasture has its own water trough, sized to fit the number of animals it accommodates.

Lucky for me—and convenient for the humans, of course—the water troughs are all on the barn side of fences. All speedily checked.

Worse and worse. A dead bird could have occurred naturally but a deceased rodent in the next? I think not. Time for my human charges to realize what's been done and get this mess cleaned up.

* * *

Avery looked down at the cat with his claws in the hem of her jeans. He'd been twining through her legs and 'talking' to her more and more urgently while she helped Camp lay out the fiber. He didn't often eat with her in the evenings. She supposed the activity around the barn had caught his interest. Unlike the horses, her own mealtimes were never on any kind of schedule.

"You were the one who decided to stow away on the ride to town, mister. Leanne or Tucker might have taken pity and fed you if you'd been here. I'll be done here shortly and we'll eat."

In response, Callahan walked his front paws up the denim of her jeans, stretching his full length along her leg.

"Just a few more minutes." Avery reached down to rub the cat's ears and found her hand snagged lightly by an unsheathed claw. "Hey," she said softly, "what's up with you?"

As those intelligent eyes stared up into hers, she accepted that the cat's mind wasn't on his stomach, for once.

Camp seemed to have reached the same conclusion as he said, "I think we'd better see what this guy wants."

Callahan dropped to four paws at the statement and once again had Avery wondering—truly wondering—if the cat, rather than acting on intonation as most animals did, understood their actual words. It should have been an eerie thought, but somehow it wasn't.

She supposed it would have looked odd to an observer for the two humans to fall in step behind the cat, picking up their pace as—after a glance back to ascertain their obedience—he began to trot toward the closest field. She couldn't help but be glad that none of her team were around to witness.

Moments later, she forgot how silly they might have appeared as she stared in horror at the dead animal floating inches below the surface of the water. Not a bird, her mind registered. That would have been a concern but it did happen from time to time. They kept bleach handy because diseased birds sought water and sometimes perished in their attempt to drink. But never had she seen a rat drown in one of the troughs.

"I need to check the other fields," she said numbly.

Appearing to be satisfied that he had their attention focused in the right direction, Callahan no longer attempted to lead or corral them but kept pace as she and Camp walked in silence from one pasture and one trough to the next. She was sickened as they found one dead animal after another floating in the water that was critical to the horses' well-being.

At the last tub, she turned to Camp and said slowly, "This doesn't fit. Nothing fits together. It's almost as if I'm dealing with two different threats."

Camp nodded. "This is more along the lines of childish temper. Like your tack being slashed by your ex. Nothing as dangerous as bullets fired."

For a moment, she wanted to agree but it was worse than Camp, who didn't know the world of horses, could realize at first glance. "This is very dangerous to the animals. Horses won't drink contaminated water. That's why I won't use self-watering systems, though that technology has become much better in recent years. We check each water source every single day."

"So, this was done at some point during the last twenty-four hours?" Camp sounded dubious.

"Maybe less than that but I'll have to check with Leanne and Tucker. In the summer, they sometimes check morning and night. Whoever did this intentionally put every horse out here at a real risk of a blocked gut and colic. Colic kills more horses than almost any other health issue. And that—the threat to the horses—is the part that doesn't fit."

Camp raised his brow questioningly as Avery hesitated.

She suspected her next revelation might give the kiss of death to her dream of adding a veteran therapy program to the ranch lineup. "Sheriff Farley says Eddie has angered people he should never have mixed with. Ben ... the sheriff ... thinks he may be desperate to pay what he owes them. We agree Eddie may be a threat to me because he'd always hoped he could later convince Marla to help him out with money, but he needs the horses. He needs the cash they represent. I don't see contaminated water being something he'd risk, not even to strike at me."

* * *

Smart girl. That was information Camp needs so that he's not chasing a rabbit down an empty hole. There's much more to all of this than even I initially thought might be. However, as the next step here—as I understand it once the dead varmints are removed—is to sanitize the tubs with great quantities of bleach, I'll take myself off. The strong odor of bleach has an unpleasant effect on my sense of smell and that would interfere much too much with enjoying my next meal, although I doubt that's *going to happen anytime soon!*

* * *

After helping Avery disinfect and scrub the water troughs, Camp went back to work on the wiring while she refilled each tub with clean water. He heard the sound of Tucker's diesel returning, so wasn't surprised when the young man rejoined him. He filled the younger man in on the dead creatures that had been deposited in every water trough and—recalling what Avery had said about the health threat to the animals—wasn't at all surprised by the low, vicious curses the vet uttered.

"Sorry, but that's pretty low to a snake's belly," Tucker concluded.

"Agreed." Camp climbed down from positioning the last camera. "I don't suppose your rounds with the neighbors turned up anything."

"Actually, yeah, but nothing I can take to the sheriff as a problem. Guy on a fancy motorcycle, lots of chrome. Heard mention of him at two different places."

"Motorcycle?" Something tugged at Camp's memory.

"Yeah, but one said Harley, one said Goldwing. Go figure. At least they now know to be on the lookout and paying attention to the details. Strangers attract attention in an outlying rural area like this." He shot Camp a look. "You have, at any rate. And Inghram was noticed as well but mostly because of that ridiculously fancy rig he was driving."

They shared a smile but it was brief, and Camp's next question was dead serious. "If someone wanted to scare Ms. Wilson—really scare her—where would they strike?"

"Marla or Jack," Tucker said without hesitation. "Marla's pretty savvy, and she'll be watchful and cautious. And Avery will be just down the hall from her and even more careful. And I'll be sleeping—and sleeping lightly—within hearing of Jack's barn, and Leanne plans to be right at his stall door."

Camp suspected he, himself, wouldn't be sleeping much at all. He wasn't entirely sure what was going on, or who was behind it, or why, but he *was* sure he didn't like it.

* * *

As I head out to the tent I share with Dax, Camp falls in step with me, which I find interesting. He doesn't appear to be following me, just seems to know where we're going, which also is interesting. The sun is long gone but his night vision seems up to the quick pace. I've no idea what his purpose might be, but humans do what humans do and it isn't always understandable.

Dax stands up at our approach. His body stills, and he waits, watching as we get close to him.

* * *

"May I?" Camp gestured at the tarp that Dax had spread over the grass in front of his pup tent.

"Yes, sir."

Camp sat cross-legged. When Dax followed suit, the cat sat next to him, upright and alert, his eyes gleaming yellow in the dark. Camp wasn't surprised when Dax remained silent. The ball was in Camp's court, and the younger man was simply waiting for the volley his way.

"Not a fan of the bunkhouse?"

"Nothing against it," Dax said, "but me and Callahan like it better out here … under the stars."

"I imagine I'd feel the same," Camp admitted. "I understand you haven't been here long."

"I'm not anywhere for long."

Camp couldn't place his accent but it wasn't local, and he said as much.

"No, sir, not local."

His goal wasn't to badger Dax, and he decided to try a different tack. A straightforward one. "I'd guess you have a fairly unbiased opinion of the people here."

Dax hesitated. "I haven't been here all that much longer than you. Maybe a week or so. Not long enough to form an opinion."

"What about first impressions? Anything or anyone feel off to you in the time you've been here?"

Dax shook his head. "No, sir. Can't say that anyone has. They've all been fair and decent. Ms. Avery might be a little too easy on some folk, and Ms. Marla might be a little too hard on some."

"And Tucker?"

"Tucker and Leanne just seem glad to work here, and they both work hard and tend to their own business, not telling everyone what they're doing wrong."

Camp nodded, not giving away he'd caught what Dax hadn't said. Apparently, Dax had been at the wrong end of Marla's temper over something not done to her satisfaction. Camp already knew she took both her responsibilities and her loyalty to Avery very seriously, maybe too seriously at times.

"Nothing else you can think of?"

"No, sir."

Camp stood to go before he outstayed his welcome. "Army?"

Dax got to his feet as well and nodded.

"And rank?"

"Sergeant."

"Thank you for your service, Sergeant."

"And thank you for yours as well."

* * *

Dax isn't exactly perturbed but he doesn't seem too happy either. "Callahan, I'm starting to think this wasn't the best place to stop awhile."

I tend to agree, but we're here and nothing to do about that now.

Dax understands the dilemma as he sighs and says, "But it won't look good if we head out now."

He's right, of course. It wouldn't look good at all. Dax could well fall under suspicion if he isn't already. That kind of thing can, and does, happen to innocent people given the right circumstances. I saw how intensely Dax was questioned not long after I met him at Franklin D. Roosevelt's personal retreat in Warm Springs, Georgia. With a man murdered in the museum of The Little White House, it wasn't a good place or time to be caught loitering, which Dax certainly was. So here we are and here we stay, which is fine with me as I have a great curiosity about how this will turn out. And I won't mind a bit helping to put another sleazeball behind bars, especially if that sleazeball is Eddie Danson. People who don't like cats can't be trusted, and one thing our kind always recognizes is a human who doesn't like us.

Chapter 7

Avery awakened to a feeling of absolute panic. She sat up, waiting and listening as remnants of menacing dreams brushed through her mind. She forced herself to control her breathing, which helped slow the rushed pumping of blood through her veins. Soft morning light filtered through the sheer curtains at her windows proving it was later than she normally slept even though she didn't feel rested.

Moments later, coffee mug in hand, she stood in front of the small but crystal-clear monitors grouped on her kitchen wall. Instead of displaying the interior of each barn, foaling stalls in particular, they were now focused outward toward the wide barn doors, all of them still solidly closed and barred from the inside. The small side doors now had padlocks, and only she and her team had keys. She disliked, intensely, the need to keep their working horses up at night and knew she couldn't let this go on forever. Still, knowing they were securely inside, had allowed her a few hours of actual sleep ... maybe not enough, but a few.

It was, she mused, a good thing that none of the pregnant mares were close to term. Besides, Tucker didn't believe any of them were at risk. Those were the ones he brought in for foaling. Avery kept her animals as close to their natural element as she could. In truth, over the years, the foaling stalls and monitors had been used more often for injury or illness than for foaling. And, thank goodness, both injury and illness were rare. Vaccinations were kept current, feed was strictly regimented, and new horses were quarantined before being assimilated into pastures with the others. Both did sometimes happen, though.

That led her back to the tainted water troughs and the staggering reminder that the danger which had woven its way through her dreams in the pre-dawn hours was a real and tangible threat.

Sighing, she pulled her thoughts from the silent monitors to the view beyond the glass door leading to her garden. The first hint of sunrise edged the horizon, a faint tinge of pink brushing what promised to be a clear sky. When plush fur brushed against her bare calf, she glanced down at the cat who'd sat at her doorstep, waiting to be let in, which she'd done while the coffee brewed. Without a doubt, he'd invaded her life along with a militaristic human. Both were easy on the eye, but—on the unfortunate side— both were very much alpha males. Not what she would have wanted or needed pushing into what she'd planned to be a quiet, single life devoted to the horses and the people who needed her help. But now? She leaned her head against the cool glass of the door.

Somehow, she had to return her ranch to normal operation, but her hope that Eddie would give up and go away had been supplanted by the realization that he had introduced some unknown and potentially treacherous elements into her life. Ben's warning, like his concern, had been crystal clear. Not Avery alone, but her horses and perhaps everyone around her, were all at risk.

Still, she couldn't spend every moment fretting. She, as well as Tucker and Leanne, had appointments with clients most of the day, and they needed to spend some time with the yearlings as well.

After a quick check of her phone calendar, she sent a brief text to Camp that she'd unlocked the garden door for him to access the coffee pot and headed to the shower.

Thirty minutes later she emerged to find him comfortably at home in her kitchen, sliding a second perfectly cooked omelet from skillet to plate. She assumed it was the second because Callahan appeared to be enjoying the first. The cat deigned to lift his head to give her an accusatory glance. She surmised he remained completely unimpressed with her meal planning.

She looked back at Camp and tried not to enjoy the sight of him standing at her stovetop. "Good morning."

He handed her the omelet. "Good morning to you. You didn't sleep well." It wasn't a question.

Ouch. "That bad, huh?" But she didn't have to ask. Her mirror had shown her the dark circles under her eyes as she'd skimmed her hair back into a pony tail to keep it from twining into ringlets by mid-morning.

Camp smiled and she wondered inanely how a man

with a high-ranking military career and all the burdens that entailed could have such pleasing laugh lines at the corners of his eyes. Those eyes seemed to be studying her appreciatively, despite the evidence of her restless night. Instead of answering her question, he asked about her schedule for the day.

"We've all got tight appointments today and tomorrow. Leanne's and Tucker's are all with clients. I have some clients later but also some workouts on horses that shouldn't be idle too long." She didn't add that she needed to make up for the lost time spent with her attorney and in court and simply dealing with the drama of Eddie. More than that, she needed the routine, needed her horses, craved the quiet structure of an orderly life, craved, too, to hear that she would be approved for the next step in the future she had planned for the ranch. "I suppose you have research to do, papers to fill out, all of that."

As a ploy to determine which direction Camp would rule, it failed as all he did was nod and agree he had things to take care of as well.

They ate in surprisingly companionable silence until her phone rang. She glanced at the caller ID before answering. "Mr. Girard, good morning."

* * *

Camp tried not to eavesdrop but Avery was listening so intently and looking sadder by the minute. Sad but not alarmed, so his first protective instinct relaxed at the realization this was not some new threat.

"Of course, Mr. Girard, you're welcome to bring Owen to say good-bye. We'll miss both of you. Yes, it does sound like a wonderful opportunity, those kinds of promotions don't get handed out every day."

Camp refilled her coffee, adding the unrefined sugar and dash of cream she preferred. She gave him a hint of smile, but it was clear her mind remained with the conversation.

"I'm glad you're going to continue with riding lessons for Owen. I agree they've done him a world of good and he's already got such quiet, skilled hands. He's made tremendous progress."

She twisted her mug. "Yes, as a matter of fact, I *have* heard of Marbleson Farms. They're a reputable facility. No. I'm sorry but you have it right, I don't sell my horses."

Camp watched her eyes as she finished the conversation and looked up at him. The sadness lingered as she sighed and said, "I've got to pull my team together for a joint decision."

"Should I leave?" he asked.

For a moment, she studied him, and he wondered what she was thinking, but then she shrugged. "It doesn't matter. It isn't a secret. I just need their input."

He leaned back in his chair as Avery made quick calls to her team, telling himself his interest was because of the bearing on his investigation. Everything he learned about the operation of the facility could have import of some sort or another.

Avery made a second carafe of coffee in the few minutes it took Marla, Leanne, and Tucker to reach her kitchen. Without answering any of the questions as they came in the door one by one, she moved them to the dining table so they could face each other as Tucker, the last to arrive, stepped into the house.

Taking a deep breath, Avery explained the phone call she'd received, finishing by saying, "Mr. Girard plans to buy a horse for Owen. I expect Marbleson Farms is completely capable of helping them select a safe animal."

Tucker nodded, his blue eyes glinting behind wire-framed glasses. "Alabama? On the Eastern Shore of Mobile Bay? They're more than reputable. I've been there a couple of times. It's a neat place. I'd be more than willing to waive the fee on a pre-purchase exam."

Avery smiled, but Camp noted the shadows hadn't left her eyes. "I'm sure that would be appreciated and very helpful."

"But unnecessary, right?" Leanne had her elbow propped on the table, chin in hand, a keen insight lighting her features.

"Perhaps, but that depends on what each of you has to say about my thoughts. You know how hard it was for Owen to learn to trust Silver Dollar. And, naturally, Mr. Girard is concerned about the hardship of this move to a new town on the boy. Coupled with new surroundings, starting over with another horse could prove a real setback for him. But we don't sell horses, and we never will."

Marla was second to catch on. She nodded slowly and her lips curved in the closest Camp had come to seeing her smile. "Ah … a gift."

But it was to Tucker, Camp noted, that Avery turned for final confirmation. The Connemara was in his barn, was his charge, as was young Owen. Camp supposed he would know best of anyone if this would be right for Silver Dollar as well as for the little boy.

Slowly Tucker nodded. "It's a good decision," he said agreed. "I'll haul our girl there whenever they're ready for her, meet with the barn manager, and make sure everyone knows what they need to know to keep her well and happy."

Avery drew a deep breath and let it go on a sigh. "That's good, then. For both of them—for Owen and for Silver Dollar. The condition I'll give Mr. Girard is that actual ownership of Silver Dollar remains with us. When it's time for Owen to step up in size, or for her to retire, she comes back to us for a well-earned old age in comfort."

* * *

A few hours later, Avery watched as Owen slowly exited his father's truck, reluctance apparent in every line of his young body as he walked toward the paddock where Tucker held Silver Dollar's lead line. The Connemara stood quietly watching and waiting as she'd been taught to do with her young charge. Most of their horses were encouraged to walk toward the clients, but the team had realized early on that it caused Owen discomfort so the ball, so to speak, was always in his court.

Owen's father moved to stand beside Avery as his son entered the paddock and carefully closed the gate behind him. Avery smiled at the man briefly but immediately shifted her attention to the boy and the horse and the young vet.

"He knows he's come to say good-bye," his father told Avery quietly. "He's decided not to ride today. He just wants to be with her."

Owen stopped some few feet away from the pretty gray, and Tucker spoke to him so quietly that Avery had to listen closely to hear.

"Good morning, Owen."

The boy nodded without speaking. He rarely spoke and, on those occasions that he did, it was to the Connemara and sometimes through her to communicate with Tucker. It appeared to Avery that his entire body leaned ever so slightly toward the little horse, but his feet remained anchored in the soft dirt of the paddock.

"Silver Dollar and I heard you were going to a grand new home," Tucker said the words almost in a croon. "You'll be close to the beach, there. Did you know that Connemaras like Silver Dollar are island ponies?"

Again, Owen nodded, this time taking a half step toward the mare.

"I think it'd be unfair if this girl didn't have the chance to get closer to the water, don't you? And I think she'd be much too lonely without you if we were to keep her *here* while you're *there*. She loves you, you know."

Owen's father laid his hand on Avery's arm where it rested against the fence. "What? What's he saying?"

Avery turned to face him then, saw the hope and the fear. "I don't sell my horses, Mr. Girard, but I find I must sometimes give them where they're needed most. Your son needs Silver Dollar, and I wouldn't be a bit surprised if Silver Dollar didn't need him every bit as much. She's timid with most of our clients but she's been nothing but confident with Owen."

Avery looked away from the tears in the man's eyes as she fought her own. The sight of the child with both arms now wrapped around Silver Dollar's neck was a bittersweet happiness. Bittersweet that modern medicine could not cure Owen, but happiness that his progress proved there was hope for his future. And happiness, too, that her team had been able to give him a gift and, in giving, prevent a heartbreak that would have been very real for him.

She felt the intensity of a stare on her and glanced around to find Camp watching her with an unfathomable expression. He may have been wondering why she would give away a part of what she had fought so hard to keep, but—if that were the case and he didn't understand— nothing she could say would help to clarify.

* * *

Things have been hopping around here this morning. It's been hard to keep an eye on every quarter. Even a cat can't be in multiple barns and paddocks at once. I hope Camp is as watchful as I think him to be, although his focus does give the impression that his thoughts are pretty single-mindedly with Avery. It's telling, though, that the lady in question seems oblivious to the fact … or giving a good pretense of it.

Marla is hard at work on the computer with a list of purchase requests she gathered from Tucker and Leanne for their respective barns. Avery added an item or two, and off Marla went. Even an hour later, my peek in the window showed her still hard at work, though she'd moved on from the pictures that denote vendor websites to a screen where she entered numbers at a steady pace. Keeping up with the paperwork for a venture like this one would have to require great care.

With Camp keeping his attention on Avery as she grooms, exercises, and cools one equine athlete after another, I've taken several turns through the barns. The cameras are handy at night when access to the barns is limited, but I don't see them as having much value with so many non-ranch persons, clients as they're called, in and about. Yet all remains quiet.

* * *

Camp hid his surprise when Marla, newly emerged from the house, joined him at the fence. She hadn't shown any interest in making him feel welcome or initiating small talk, not that he thought she should. Today, however, she propped a worn but quality work boot on the lower fence rail as if she planned to be there for a while.

Since he'd been given the opportunity, he took it, introducing a topic he knew would get Eddie's daughter talking. "The mare she gave away this morning, the Connemara, was she a rescue horse, too?"

Marla gave him a quick glance, as if wondering that he felt the need to talk to her. "Yes, but not from a kill pen. Some freaking Californian with more money than sense decided it would be lovely to own a pony from Ireland so she bought Silver Dollar and had her shipped over. Stupid bitch didn't realize there would be several weeks of quarantine and testing for diseases before Silver Dollar touched American soil or that the expense of it would be out of her bank account. She got bored before the end of the quarantine period and left Silver Dollar to her fate. Somehow the pony got hurt during the quarantine, and the authorities couldn't find anyone to adopt her and take on the vet expenses necessary for her treatment. Avery got wind of her days before she would have been put down. We drove cross country to get her with Avery checking in with the officials every few hours to make sure every shift and every person there knew we were headed that way so they wouldn't go ahead with the killing."

"That was a long drive to pick up a horse that might not have worked out."

Marla shrugged. "It wouldn't have mattered. That wasn't why we went. But Silver Dollar was a good addition to the ranch, and she'll be hard to replace. Still, Avery did the right thing, and we're all glad for that."

Like Camp, her attention was still fixed on Avery who had brought the fast canter of a short, stocky horse to a sudden stop and now had him spinning circles with the lightest touch of her feet to his sides, her hands perfectly centered and still on the reins.

"She's working it off." When he didn't respond, Marla returned his sideways look and elaborated. "It's what Avery does when she's worried or stressed more than she can handle. She gets on a horse and makes each one do what they were trained to do. And she always finds that thing they love during the training, that one thing they're best at doing. But it's still work for them and for her."

It was, he recalled, almost verbatim, what Avery had said about Marla herself. "Is that what you were doing yesterday afternoon? Working it off?"

"A bit, I suppose, but mine was more anger than worry."

So, Avery had gotten that aspect of it right as well. The two women knew each other well, but he supposed that was to be expected.

"I won't have him torment her like this," Marla said. "He was stupid, and it cost him. He can get over it or not, but I won't let him make her life a complete misery."

"Strong words from a daughter."

Marla turned to face him, propping her elbows on the paddock fence behind her. Camp might have thought the pose deliberately provocative had her lips not remained pressed thin and her stare challenging and even a little hostile. He could understand that hostility and didn't take it personally.

"I'm *her* daughter, too, maybe even more than his. He hasn't been much of a father in the past few years. I'm nothing more than another means to an end to him."

"How so?"

At his question, her expression became more guarded. "It doesn't matter. All Eddie, and *you*, need to know is I'll do whatever I need to do to keep Avery safe and this place safe *for* her."

"You see me as a threat?"

"Not at all," she said dismissively as she pushed away from the fence. She strode away without a backward glance.

* * *

Well, well, well. That was an interesting exchange. There seemed some point to Marla's conversational gambit, but I'm not at all sure I know what that point was other than to put Camp in his place where Avery is concerned. Judging by Camp's expression as he watches her depart, he's as perplexed—and unimpressed—as I am.

Chapter 8

Avery unsaddled then brushed Jingle. The hard work of the morning had helped ease the sense of doom she'd felt hanging over her. There was nothing more soothing to her than the familiar tasks that she loved. To her frustration, the bit of peace she'd gained had been eroded by the sight of Marla's departing stride—and Camp staring after her. She hadn't missed, either, those few minutes when the two had been face to face in deep conversation. Marla's back had been to her, but Camp's expression had been one of intense interest in whatever thoughts she'd been sharing with him. Avery didn't allow herself the luxury of analyzing why that nipped at her. It didn't matter. She couldn't let it. No matter what the discussion, she knew Marla was always in her corner. And Camp was there to do a job, then leave.

It stung that the job he'd come to do was to judge this place she loved so much and into which she'd poured her heart, soul, sweat, and tears. Not just judging the buildings and the horses, but her and the team who'd worked so hard right along with her. And it stung all the more that it was taking him such a long time to make his decision. He'd only been here a couple of days, true, but he had to have done his homework before he got this far. Anything less would have been a wasted trip. She couldn't imagine Camp Kirkland wasting effort in any direction.

Jingle nudged her, and she rubbed his neck affectionately before walking him back to his stall. "You're right," she murmured to the horse. "Marla's an adult. Her business is her own."

Giving Jingle a handful of treats, she kissed his forehead, hung his halter on the hook outside his door. Then she stepped around the corner to his older sibling's stall. Jangle, the seven-year-old son of a thoroughbred mare, was his exact opposite in looks. She and her team marveled that every one of Jack's offspring carried the physical genetics of the dam but—more importantly—the mental and emotional characteristics of Jack. They learned quickly, loved to work, and were blessed with a natural affinity for people who needed them. Every one of them had shown his amazing ability to connect with damaged humans. And, so far, none had been born a filly which was an oddity in itself.

Jangle was close to sixteen hands with the lean muscles of his thoroughbred mother but none of that breed's potential for flightiness. He was as solid as the rock he looked to be. Avery ran her hands along the leather of the bridle, then the stirrups and front and back girths. It was as automatic for her to check for signs of wear on saddle leather as it was to breathe. They couldn't afford to take chances with the safety of any of their clients, some of whom were at the very beginning of their horse experience. She and her team cleaned and maintained all of the tack meticulously but Avery insisted upon a full check before any clients were mounted. She did the same for herself, almost religiously, to set that good example.

She positioned several low jumps before snugging the cinch and swinging into the saddle, aware of Camp still there, still watching. She wasn't used to an audience and found it more than a little disconcerting. Even so, she carefully put Camp's presence from her mind and gave her full attention to Jangle. He was a joy to ride. Jumping would never be her preference in riding, but the gelding loved it, and she'd learned to handle the low jumps for his sake.

She took the small hurdles all slow and easy, letting Jangle set the pace, letting him choose when to soar over each. Her job was more to stay out of his way. Unlike Jingle, who still needed her help, this sibling knew what to do and when to do it.

It wasn't until the third round of jumps that she felt something slip in the saddle beneath her. Her heart dropped at the unexpected sensation of insecurity. She sensed when Jangle felt it, as well, but it was too late for either to react. They were in the air and all Avery could do was try her best to stay centered until he landed. She quickly realized she wasn't going to be successful. Her thought as the ground flew up to meet her was that at least they were clear of the jump.

The landing took the breath from her and, for a moment, she was completely dazed as she stared up at blue sky. She heard Camp's shout of concern, and wanted to tell him not to startle the gelding, but there was no breath in her lungs for the words.

Then Camp was crouched over her, looking into her eyes and telling her not to move. She would've laughed if she could because moving wasn't an option until she could breathe again.

When her breath did come back to her it was almost as painful as having it knocked out. Almost. She pushed to her elbows.

"I need to get up." Her voice sounded weak even to her.

"You need to be still until I figure out how badly you're hurt."

Ignoring Camp, she sat. "Bruised, maybe. Where's Jangle? Something happened."

At her movement, the gelding stepped toward her, and she realized he'd stopped in his tracks as soon as she landed. Camp reached up to take the reins so the animal couldn't come any closer.

"Whoa, fella. It won't help if you step on her." He gave Avery his arm to brace herself as she pulled to her feet. "You're a hard-headed woman."

She didn't hear any admiration in the comment so accepted it for the scold it was without responding. When she reached for the reins, Camp released them. She watched as he picked up the saddle and carried it over to the fence rail. When he had his back to her, she bent forward at the waist, pulling in air, but she kept that show of weakness brief. While Camp was absorbed in studying the saddle, she checked Jangle, carefully walking alongside him. He didn't show any sign of injury from what could have been an awkward landing. Only when she was satisfied with his well-being did she follow Camp to the rail, where he examined the English saddle she'd been using.

He glanced up at her approach. "Do all of the horses have their own saddles?"

That seemed an odd question to her. "Most, yes, because they have different jobs. Some, because not every saddle fits every horse. Sometimes we have to swap out for rider size. We can adjust stirrup lengths, but if a rider needs a larger or smaller seat, that can't be adjusted." She studied the saddle, trying to see what he saw. "Why do you ask?"

Camp's expression was grim as he asked, "Who else was likely to ride in this saddle?"

"Just me or Marla. Leanne's never gotten comfortable riding English even though Jangle's in her barn."

Since Camp hadn't answered her question, Avery moved in closer, knowing she wasn't going to like anything she saw and she was right. The leather she'd checked so carefully was intact, but the steel girth ring was broken through.

"I don't understand," she said bewildered. "This saddle isn't new but it isn't all that old, either. And I've never seen that happen before."

"It was filed thin." Camp turned the backside of the metal piece toward her. "See on either side of the break? You can tell some kind of file was used to wear through the metal."

"A rasp," Avery said numbly. "Most likely a farrier's rasp."

"Is that something you keep here?"

"Yes. We don't do our own horses' feet but occasionally we have to rasp and pull nails from a shoe to prevent additional damage from a partially pulled shoe until the farrier can get here."

Avery stared at the damaged ring, feeling the heavy thud of her own heartbeat. She wasn't concerned with the risk to herself but the thought that someone would put a client—a client living with or recovering from emotional or physical limitations—at risk like this made her nauseous. That took a very sick sort of person.

"I don't know what to do." The comment slipped out before she thought. Never would she have willingly revealed that kind of weakness and uncertainty to him. Or anyone else.

* * *

Camp turned to look at her and the harsh angles of his expression eased. "You're going to call the sheriff and warn your team. Have them look at every saddle in every barn for similar damage. I'm going to make some calls of my own." Almost as if he couldn't help himself, he brushed at some sand on her face. His touch was light, gentle. "Are you okay to take care of your horse?"

Fighting the impulse to lean her cheek into his touch, Avery straightened her shoulders. "I'm fine." And she would be. She was used to doing what had to be done and what had to be done was rarely quick or easy.

She felt Camp's gaze on her as she walked away. She tried not to limp but she could already feel the stiffness that would get worse before it got better. Her lips twisted wryly. She didn't suppose her stride looked nearly as attractive as Marla's had a short time before.

* * *

Here I'd thought things couldn't get much uglier, but they just did. Tossing dead critters in a few water troughs is little more than a prank compared to this. Avery could have been crippled or killed under the hooves of an animal that size. His gentleness couldn't have saved her, and he really is a gentle giant. Some of the other horses are a bit feisty and that requires watching. It may seem like great fun to chase a cat through a darkened pasture, but it's not fun to be on the receiving end. It was, in fact, demeaning to have to make a run for my life but that was where I found myself last night while doing a bit of recon. Youngsters have a peculiar sense of play.

But this—a saddle deliberately damaged to fail during use—is deadly. Not child's play at all.

And I find myself almost in the same jam as Avery in not knowing what to do next. The cameras won't be useful unless someone attempts to break into one of the barns at night. I have to hope we get that lucky as these midnight rounds are getting tiresome. We need a break soon. I guess I'll hang with Camp a bit, see if he has any ideas that I can put to good use with or without him.

I find him pacing the wide front porch—verandah some call it—and talking on that cell phone of his. I do wish these humans would realize how difficult it is to eavesdrop. The distance to the ground is difficult enough. Being forced to keep up with the strides of an agitated human male while listening is added frustration.

"You're right, this is important. I know I don't often ask for favors. There's a reason for that as you damn well know. Payback is always hell with you."

Ah, a chuckle, that's encouraging. I thought this was a disagreement of some sort.

"Yeah, work your magic. The sheriff's on it, but I'm not sure what he'll share with me even if he does manage to dig something up. I need to know who her ex is in debt to and how much he's in for."

I'm glad when he stops pacing for a moment. The conversation will be a lot easier to follow.

"No, I wouldn't lay odds on her guilt or innocence over the missing checks, but there's something going on here a hell of a lot bigger than that. It seems straightforward enough that her ex got himself up to his eyeballs in some kind of gambling thing. He obviously planned to pay it off selling the ranch and the horses. The judge's ruling in the divorce put an end to any hopes he had of that."

He resumes his pacing. This restless energy is uncharacteristic of what I've seen since his arrival on the ranch.

He scowls and stops again. "Don't worry about how I feel. It won't change the outcome of my investigation here."

Ha, I detect more than a little attitude from Camp. Whoever he's conversing with has touched a sore spot, and that uncomfortable spot is Avery.

"Can't disagree with you on that. If he got her deep enough in debt, she might have signed off on those fraudulent checks and split the difference with Cassidy on our end."

Oh, now, that's not right! Fraudulent checks? He better not suspect Avery of wrong-doing! Now I'm on the wrong side of both Camp and whoever he's talking with. I thought Camp had better insight than that!

"BS on that. I'd rather pay you in dollars. Yeah, yeah, I know—you'll get it back in spades. Just come through for me on this. I've got the ranch covered, but I need boots on the ground elsewhere. One more thing, check on a Neal Tarent for me. I don't know how he plays into all this, but I need to know if he's a real bad-ass or a wannabe. Hey, and thanks, okay?"

All right then, so Camp is calling in reinforcements. That's a good thing. His suspicions of Avery, however, are a bad thing. I'll have to do what I can to lessen this misperception. One thing I'm sure of is that Avery is not the Bonnie to her ex-husband's Clyde.

* * *

Camp walked through Avery's small garden and knocked on the side entrance of her house, long past lights-out at the ranch. As soon as she opened it, he said brusquely, "You shouldn't be opening the door this time of night without checking to see who's on the other side."

She shrugged. "If you didn't want me to answer, you shouldn't have knocked. But I saw you headed this way through the office window. I've been going over more of the mountains of accounts Marla makes me read and approve for her. Besides, Callahan went to investigate without yowling, so I knew it had to be more friend than foe approaching."

Camp suspected from her smile that she wasn't sure she could count him as a friend or even neutral. As smiles went, it was wary and weary and barely friendly, but at least she wasn't glaring at him. He'd have to be happy with that.

He nodded pointedly at the glass of wine she held in her hand. "Got more of that?"

Although she seemed momentarily surprised, she moved back from the door. "Sure. Come on in."

He stepped in and pulled the door closed behind him. They stood for a heartbeat looking at each other and the silence of the moment enveloped him. He liked the way she looked in workout pants as much as he liked her in jeans. He especially liked the way she had her hair piled on top of her head, damp tendrils curling against her neck.

Avery was the one to break the silence, and he suspected it was altogether deliberate. "White or red?"

"Either."

She paused in the process of taking another wine glass from the cabinet and gave him a long look. "Would you prefer a beer? Most people who don't care if they're drinking white or red would rather not be drinking wine at all."

"Beer, then," he said, "because you're right on that." He took a seat at the quartz bar without being asked.

She handed him a cold bottle and an opener, placed a glass in front of him. "What are you doing here this late?"

Her tone was blunt but not insulting so he decided to go with it.

"Checking on you." It was the truth—just not all of it. He ignored the glass and drank from the bottle. The beer was dark and expensive and damned good.

Instead of sitting beside him, she leaned on the countertop opposite him and sipped her wine, watching him over the top. A faint frown touched her forehead. "I'm fine."

"You were lucky."

"I suppose." Instead of taking another drink from the glass, she put its moisture-beaded surface to her forehead. "Lucky." She gave a small laugh that held absolutely no humor. "This time."

"That's pretty much my point. You may not be again. Your clients, as you call them, may not be."

"I know this doesn't look good for your review, but I swear I'll get all of this settled soon."

"How are you planning to do that? Pay off Danson's gambling debts?" He was pushing, and he knew it.

"I won't do that." She sighed. "And even if I would, I'm not sure I could. If the sheriff is right, I'm afraid they're much bigger than anything I could come up with."

Camp took another swallow of beer, savored the taste of it. "And so, what now?"

"Now, I keep doing what I do."

"You'd be wiser to take some time off, cancel appointments for a little while. Things are dicey and seem to be getting even more so."

Her eyes widened, and he felt like he was drowning in the green-gold depths of them. "Cancel appointments? I can't do that!"

He wondered at the hint of desperation in her tone and said reassuringly, "Just for a week or so until we can figure this out." He hadn't meant to say *we* and had a moment's gratitude when she didn't pick up on it.

"When I said I can't, I meant just that," she admitted reluctantly. "New Hope isn't sinking, by any means, but Eddie did put me—put the ranch—in a bind. Tucker and Leanne need their salaries, and I have feed to buy and bills to pay. I can't do all that without income from clients coming in, and I can't afford to lose those clients permanently. Many of them are referred by physicians. They need this place, what we offer. If they can't get it here, they'll have to be referred elsewhere. I'd owe them that. There are other reputable places not that far away. I've already talked to Leanne and Tucker and Marla. We'll all be extra vigilant."

Camp shook his head. "What if that—being vigilant—isn't good enough to keep you, them, and whoever the hell else, safe?"

She placed the wine glass carefully on the quartz. "Look, I don't beg—ever. I work and sweat and bleed if I have to, but I don't ask for what I don't earn. Don't write us off, please, not yet. We have so much to offer the veterans who have given everything to our country."

The words came as if wrung from her, and he could tell the cost to her pride. He wanted to reassure her, but he couldn't. "No decision yet." It was as much as he could offer. And he could tell by the disappointment in those beautiful eyes that it was no reassurance at all.

Chapter 9

A very closed the door behind Camp firmly. No matter the outcome of Camp's investigation, she *would* find a way to do what she felt driven to do. As she'd found a way to do everything else of importance to her. And she'd do it alone. Too late, she'd realized that Eddie was a deterrent more than a help to things that mattered. She'd trusted him once. Trusted him implicitly. She wouldn't give that kind of power to any man, ever again.

She couldn't help her brother, couldn't even find him, but there were other veterans who needed her, who would allow her and the horses into their lives. Those she could— and would—find a way to help, whether she was approved to participate in the government's program or not. Maybe not on as large a scale, but everything and anything she could do would count. Not Camp Kirkland or anyone else could stop her there. It might hurt that he thought her unworthy, but it wouldn't stop her.

As she emptied her wine glass and placed it in the dishwasher, she felt Callahan twining around her ankles. He was usually back with Dax by now, but when he'd asked to go out earlier, he returned within minutes to sit on the steps until she opened the door to him. She stooped to give him a rub but her fingers barely skimmed his fur as he walked from her to the glass door that led to the garden. She'd need to close the solid inner door before she turned in for the night, but she liked having it open more often than not, liked the night sky and the sense of space. There'd been a time when she'd been secure enough in this haven she'd created to leave it open as she slept, that glass the only barrier between herself and the outside world. She didn't feel that safe anymore.

The realization made her restless. When Callahan turned back to her again, she suspected he felt as agitated as she. She glanced at the monitors and found the view they gave of the barns reassuringly quiet. At least that view should have been reassuring. She still felt as uneasy as Callahan looked.

The cat gave a plaintive yowl, and she shook her head. "So, you're ready to leave now?"

But when she walked to the door, he sat in the middle of the room, watching her. "I don't have a clue what's up with you, but it's late, and you're welcome to settle in here for the night if that's what you want."

Even as she said the words, she realized she hadn't yet heard Marla come in. Marla had her own entrance to the house. A few years back, they'd created a separate living space, small but comfortable, even adding a tiny kitchenette, though Marla preferred to share meals with Avery. On most evenings, Avery could hear the sound of her moving about or perhaps it was more that she sensed another presence. But not tonight.

Avery didn't like to hover but the temptation to check on Marla was strong. She'd finish her office work first, she told herself. By then, her stepdaughter should be home so she'd give it at least that long. Marla was an adult, after all. The fact that recent events were unnerving didn't change that reality.

The damaged saddle heaped on her dining room floor was all the reminder she needed of how unnerving those events had proven. Ben Farley was sending someone to pick it up for evidence first thing tomorrow. He'd promised to have it dusted for prints, but she and the sheriff both knew there'd be nothing to find that would incriminate anyone. The prints on that saddle would belong to people who had no reason to wear gloves or wipe the saddle clean of any trace they might have left behind.

She battled her inner, and Callahan's outer, anxiety another hour before she tried Marla's number. It rang the requisite three times before going to voice mail. Avery didn't leave a message. Marla would get in touch with her as soon as she saw the missed call. She'd always been good about that, even as a teenager, certainly in the years that she and Avery had become a team.

After a quick check confirmed that Marla's car was not where she normally parked, Avery made herself accept that Marla had gone out for the evening and might or might not return that night. Still feeling unsettled, she hit the elliptical. As hard as she had worked today, stress was overriding any benefits from the activity. A workout was the one thing that might combat the ill effects of tension and her fall. She could not afford a sleepless night.

When her cell phone finally rang, she nearly fell off the exercise machine reaching to answer it.

"Marla." She didn't try to hide the relief in her voice.

Silence, then, "No, this is Leanne."

"Sorry, I didn't look at the caller ID." Avery held her concern in check. "Everything okay out there?"

"Avery, I'm not there. Marla didn't tell you?"

Avery rubbed at the sudden tightness between her brows. "I haven't talked with Marla. Tell me what?"

"She sent me home; said I hadn't been married long enough to be spending my nights in a barn alone. But Avery, I'm worried. She didn't answer my text message, so I called, and she didn't answer that either. She promised she would—that's why I agreed to let her do this. I'm already on my way but …"

Even as Leanne talked, Avery had been pulling a pair of socks from a drawer. "I'm going to the barn. I'll find her." She clicked off, not bothering to answer when Leanne rang her right back.

Avery grabbed a lightweight hoodie from the basket in her closet and headed to the mudroom where her boots waited. Callahan trotted through the darkened house at her side.

For one brief moment, she thought of calling Camp for backup, but her feelings were still stinging from their last exchange. Instead, she called Tucker who answered on the first ring. "What's up?"

"Go to Barn One. I'm looking for Marla."

* * *

Marla's vehicle was parked in the shadows close to the side entrance of the barn. Tucker waited for her there and shook his head. "Everything's quiet inside. Marla isn't there."

The fact that Marla's transportation was there, but not Marla, couldn't be a good thing. Before Avery could voice that concern, Callahan yowled once then streaked past both of them. Avery's reaction was gut-based and immediate. She couldn't recall the exact moment she'd come to trust the cat's instincts or knowledge or whatever it was that propelled him in a given direction. All she knew was that he'd displayed an uncanny accuracy for detecting trouble long before the humans around him.

Avery broke into a run right behind him, disregarding the night shadows that made speed hazardous. The flashlight Tucker snapped on did little more than disorient her with its bobbing, shifting beam. She heard Leanne's truck sliding into the gravel at Barn One, the slamming of the truck door, and Leanne's voice calling to her. She saved her breath for running, knowing Leanne would see the beam from Tucker's light and find them soon enough.

Callahan moved quickly along the fence rail that ran behind the barns, passing the wide gates of the first two pastures. At the farthest gate, he stopped briefly and yowled again, urging them to catch up before he shot forward toward the two- and three-year-old horses. Typically, they huddled together, taking comfort from each other as they slept. They were still gathered, but milled restlessly about.

Avery lost sight of Callahan momentarily. "Marla?" she heard the panic in her own voice and forced herself to take a deep breath, before calling out again.

"There!" Tucker said, lifting his flashlight. "I see the cat's eyes shining in the dark!"

* * *

Easy does it. Thank goodness for smart humans. Avery tells Tucker to turn off the flashlight and warns both him and Leanne to move slowly so as not to spook the young horses. They seem as large as adults to me but I sense their immaturity. Marla is sitting up but not moving. She may be hurt or just dazed but, either way, she's too close to those sharp hooves. These youngsters are already disturbed. Any sudden movement could send them into a panic. My speed and agility could put me over the fence easy enough, but Marla might well be trampled.

Within moments, Avery is kneeling beside Marla. While the humans evaluate the need for medical attention, I'll do some snooping on my own. Not much to tell by the appearance of the ground except that there seems to have been a scuffle of some sort. But the ground is too hard and dry for anything as clear as footprints. Not to mention the fact that the young horses have been stomping about. It will be a wonder if none of them has stepped on Marla already.

Ah, what have we here? Some sort of halter, it appears, but nothing like the quality that Avery purchases for her ranch. Instead of leather stitched to solid metal connections, this is made entirely of rope with its own lead line built in. Interesting and a pretty darn clever device. I think Camp needs to see this, and it comes as no surprise to me that he has already arrived on the scene.

* * *

"Marla, are you hurt?" Avery crouched down, careful not to bump against her stepdaughter. She looked across

Marla to Tucker who was level with her on the other side. "Tucker, we may need an ambulance."

"No," Marla said at once, but her voice sounded weak and thready to Avery's anxious mind. "I'm fine. Shaken a little and pissed a lot, but fine. He shoved my face in the dirt before he took off, probably to make sure I didn't get a better look at him."

Tucker growled and rocked back on his heels. "I'll kill the bastard for that."

"At least the pasture babies are safe. The jerk jumped the fence, so I know he didn't get any of them."

"Did you see who it was? Could you describe him?" The sound of Camp's voice so close startled Avery, but she realized almost at once that it shouldn't have. He had an uncanny ability to track misfortune.

"I wish. I'm not even real sure it was a guy, but I think so, broad shoulders and all that."

Marla's voice seemed stronger, now, Avery thought, and even more irritated. But still, she'd taken a hit and could have injuries more serious than she was aware. "Maybe you shouldn't talk right now. Let's at least get you inside and comfortable. I want to see you in the light."

"I've no doubt I look like warmed-over death with a few scrapes and bruises and a covering of dirt thrown in, but I'm fine, Avery, honest. I'm just glad I got restless in the barn and stepped out for some fresh air. The first inclination I knew that something was up was hearing the colts snort and blow. I thought maybe a coyote had gotten into the field."

"Avery?" Leanne's voice pulled her attention from Marla. "I think you need to take a look at what the cat's found."

But it was Camp who reached down and took the rope

halter from between Callahan's sharp teeth. He held it toward Avery. "Recognize this?"

"No," she said slowly. "It's not one of ours."

Anger burned through her at the realization. There was no doubt in her mind now. Someone had tried to steal one of Jack's babies and might well have succeeded if not for Marla. There was also no doubt in her mind that Tarent was behind this. Inghram wasn't the type for stealth-in-the-dark activities, but Tarent could have many on his payroll who had both the temperament and the skills. If Tarent wanted a fight, he was going to get one. She'd make damned sure of that.

* * *

Camp found himself amazed at the way Avery held to her routine the next day, even after all that had happened. Most women—hell, most men—would be in stress mode. If Avery was stressed, he couldn't tell. If anything burned in her this morning, it was probably a lingering fury.

Once she was convinced Marla wasn't seriously injured, he'd seen the anger take over. In full view and hearing of every one of them crowded into her kitchen the night before, she'd pulled up Eddie's number on her cell phone. Her warning, more of a promise than a threat to Camp's mind, had been issued in clear, concise terms.

"I didn't expect you to answer, Eddie, not when you saw my name on your screen, and that's fine, but I know you'll listen to this message. You need to hear, know, and understand something. You'd better call off your dogs—Tarent and any others—and make them believe that nothing on this property belongs to you. If anything happens—if Marla, if any of my team gets hurt or any of these horses are taken—you're going to pay way more than any debt you owe them. In fact, you'd better pray that none of my horses even come down with a cough, because I'm going to blame you and I'm going to come looking for you. Bet on it."

When she clicked off, she'd glared right at Camp as if daring him to comment. He hadn't. Nor had any of her team, though they probably wanted to applaud her as much as he did.

He watched her now as she methodically groomed a strong-looking horse that stood quietly under her attention. Camp had no doubt she was aware of his presence, but she didn't comment on the fact or so much as acknowledge him. She talked softly to the animal the whole while, resolutely ignoring the fact that Camp was watching her every movement. When the light red coat gleamed to suit her, she went over the saddle, touching every piece of it with meticulous care before swinging it up on that muscular back.

As she pulled the girth snug, an SUV pulled alongside the paddock in front of Barn Three. Camp watched a sturdy, young woman in scrubs step out of the driver's side and walk around to open the passenger door. A too-thin, young man eased his way out, leaning heavily upon a cane until he was upright, after which he used it to find his way forward. His eyes were open, but Camp realized at once that they were sightless.

Avery left the horse ground-tied and met the young man at the paddock fence. She smiled at him warmly. "Sergeant Gallagher. Good morning."

"Good morning, ma'am. How are you?"

"Happy that the sun is shining and all my horses are healthy."

"How is Applejack today?" Camp could hear the eagerness and affection in the soldier's voice. "Ready for a ride?"

"That one's always ready. He's tireless. And, yes, he's ready for you. All saddled."

"One day I want to be able to saddle him myself." Though Camp couldn't hear even a hint of self-pity in the young man's voice, his own throat tightened. Men like Sergeant Gallagher had given way too much, way too young. What a small thing that would seem to most riders, the ability to saddle their own horse. Maybe even a burden rather than a blessing that they could do so.

"And you will," Avery said evenly. "Think how far you've come in these few weeks. You can ride without me, unsaddle him, and groom him without me. A bit longer and I promise you'll saddle by yourself."

But Camp suspected that wouldn't happen until Avery was sure the sabotage had ended and the saboteur was behind bars.

Avery moved to the center of the ring, watching as the horse and rider circled her slowly. The soldier's balance was steady, and Camp knew how difficult that balance astride a horse must have been to develop without sight. He'd seen so many veterans struggle on their own two feet once they'd lost the ability to see. After fifteen or so minutes, Gallagher lifted the reins slightly which cued the horse to a slow jog. Camp wouldn't have called it a trot but definitely more than a walk. After another fifteen minutes, the soldier reined him back down to a walk and turned him in the opposite direction and started over again.

Camp's gaze stayed as much on Avery as the soldier. She talked encouragingly to him as often as she was silent. Camp never heard the least hint of weariness or impatience at the slow pace of the session. Nor did her smile, genuine and pleased, once slip.

After a bit, he supposed curiosity got the better of the nurse as she moved to stand beside him. "I haven't seen you here before. Are you a student?" Her glance was bright and friendly, her freckled face pleasing with a cheerful expression.

"No, I'm visiting. Are you with the VA?"

She pulled a face at that. "No, thank the Lord. I work at the regional hospital. I bring Sergeant Gallagher here on my own time between shifts."

That caught Camp's attention. "That's good of you."

"Little enough. I lost my husband to an IED three years back."

"I'm sorry for your loss," Camp said. "And I'm grateful for your husband's service to this country and yours to those who served." It wasn't a trite offering, never would be.

She took a deep breath as a look of sorrow crossed her face. "I do what I can for those who do make it home. A little bit like Ms. Avery, I guess. I don't know how much money she could be making with the time she donates to the veterans. She's trying to get in some government program that will pay her back for her time and maybe let her take on some more but last she mentioned it, the government was taking its usual slow crawl to get to her application. Even if it works out, I suspect she'll always give time to some that might not be covered even by that."

Camp turned his attention back to the center of the ring with way more to think about than he'd expected. He tried not to read into Avery's face what might not be there, but he couldn't deny the joy shining in her eyes, the fiercely hopeful expression on her face as she watched the soldier. Camp had fought the attraction he felt for her, knowing he had to be objective, knowing he had to see her clearly enough to know if she was capable of subterfuge, of pocketing money intended to help wounded veterans.

But now? No way, Camp thought, no way in hell could he believe she'd risk everything she'd created here for a few fraudulent dollars. No way would she jeopardize her dream of helping the men and women who put their lives on the line every day they were away from their families. Whatever was happening, she was the victim and not the catalyst behind the events.

And somehow, he had to figure out the who and the why behind what was. Eddie was the easy answer, almost too easy. And sometimes the easy answer was the correct one, but Camp would dig and dig deep—deep enough to be certain the answer he found was the true one.

Chapter 10

*T*hings are heating up and not just between Avery and Camp. The danger's increasing but so is the sneaky feeling that I'm still missing a key point.

Maybe the weak-spined ex really is behind all of the catastrophes, but why, then, haven't I scented his recent presence around any of the barns or paddocks? It lingers in some places, most recently and most strongly in the guest quarters he's said to have used through the lengthy divorce proceedings. It's in the main house as well, but fading there. I've even caught a whiff or two around the tack rooms. With that taken into consideration, I'll have to decide whether or not I can accept that the so-called spineless ex—and I don't disagree with that description—could put into play the increasingly nasty turns of events. It seems just as possible that he's a victim of his own stupidity with those nasty events no more than the domino effect of *that stupidity.*

At the center of the danger is Avery, around whom everyone seems to be hovering this morning. Camp has yet to take his eyes from her though she seems oblivious to his stare as she watches the soldier astride a massive horse. The young man, though sightless, remains determined to learn new ways to enjoy his life. Tucker has edged over from his work once or twice to check on Avery, who seems more friend and mentor than employer, as has Leanne. And here is Marla, yet again, hovering and casting anxious glances toward Avery. If possible, Marla seems even more agitated now than last night after her own brush with danger.

Marla glances down at her ringing cell phone. Her frown deepens, and I decide to step a bit closer as she answers. In my opinion, eavesdropping is less a character flaw than a tool of the trade.

"I wouldn't consider Avery's voice message a threat, if I were you. More like a promise." *Marla is angry … fighting mad, as Dax would say. Her voice sounds edgy and her pacing, as she listens to whoever is at the other end of the line, brings her closer to Camp.*

"What did you expect her to do? Let you take everything she's worked so hard to build here and squander it on your bad habits?"

Her rising tone draws Camp's interest from Avery.

"I *have* tried to help you, Dad. I don't know what else to do. I can't support myself and you and your gambling too. You've got to stop! Stay away from here, just stay away."

Marla seems to have noticed that she now has Camp's complete attention. She turns away and lowers her voice, wiping at what I suspect are tears in her eyes. Lucky for me, she seems unaware of my own quick move to keep within hearing of her conversation.

"What do you mean you're afraid? Of who?" *Marla pauses, no doubt listening to the reply.* "Jesus, Dad! Okay, yes. I'll meet you, but it won't change anything. I can't help you with this."

There's no mistaking Marla's agitation as she slides her phone into her pocket. This isn't likely to end well for anyone.

I wish Camp had heard more of that conversation. At the same time, I'm glad that Avery remained focused on her client. She doesn't need anything else to stress her, and I suspect Marla plans to place herself in the line of fire with her mix of anger at and worry for her father.

* * *

"What's next on your agenda?"

Avery pulled her gaze from the young sergeant as he carefully unsaddled Applejack. She glanced briefly at Camp, before returning her attention to her client. It alarmed as much as irritated her to realize that she found Camp more appealing each day. "I've got a contractor coming out to talk with me later today."

"Contractor? Are you starting another barn?"

"No. It's a project I've had in mind for a long time. The problem is the work is already started, but this guy is dragging his heels about finishing. I've asked him to meet with me, but I've got a few hours before he'll be here. I'll put that time into paperwork."

"I've got a better idea. Let's go into town for some lunch. It will do you good to get away from here for a couple of hours."

For a moment, Avery stared at him. Was he … what? Asking her for a date? Wanting to grill her again? Rather than stand there and wonder, she asked bluntly, "Why?"

His smile was killer—at least for her—she admitted to herself.

"Just because," he said, his tone light and easy. "We've

got to eat. We both have time. You can tell me about this new project you've got going."

Telling herself she was batshit crazy for so much as considering it, she found herself nodding assent all the same. The idea appealed to her. Camp appealed to her, damn it. "I'll have to get things cleared away from this session and Applejack back in his stall. But … okay."

She smiled as she watched Sergeant Gallagher curry and brush Applejack. She loved seeing the care he took, the affection in every stroke. They scheduled his next appointment, before she said good-bye to him and to the nurse who volunteered to drive him faithfully each week. Avery wondered sometimes if the nurse had feelings for the soldier, feelings that went beyond being a Good Samaritan. But it was none of her business, and she had plenty on her plate without worrying whether or not two hurting souls might find real and lasting joy in each other.

Thoughts of Camp returned as she walked toward the house, and she had to wonder if she truly had lost her mind, to not just brush the dust from her clothes and grab her purse but to change into something a bit nicer, a bit more flattering. She dusted some blush across her cheeks to take the pallor away and added a bit of color to her lips.

When she was done, she stood at the bathroom sink and stared at herself in the mirror. She didn't look old, she acknowledged, but she felt old. Eddie had made her feel unattractive, something brushed aside and of far less importance to him than his addiction. It might almost have been easier if he'd had some grand and passionate affair, left her to be with another woman. She wasn't sure why that was so, but she felt that being set aside for a living, breathing creature was something she could have understood. He hadn't cared for his string of flirtations any more than he'd cared for her. They, like she, had been found less enticing than a game of blackjack.

And as she had that thought, she had another. It no longer hurt. All that Eddie had done or said in the past years had lost the power to hurt. She smiled at herself in the mirror and suddenly felt a bit pretty again. Lord, it had been a long time since she'd felt attractive.

"Batshit crazy," she told the face in the mirror, but when she turned away, she was still smiling.

* * *

It was nice to feel Camp's hand on her elbow as she stepped up into the passenger seat of his truck and she decided to let it feel good, at least for now, at least for a little while. He'd be gone soon but she could allow herself to enjoy this feeling, however fleeting it might be. Her reality, though, was that while her past life with Eddie no longer had the power to hurt her emotionally, his misdeeds could hurt her in ways far worse. She'd have to focus on damage control to survive, to ensure her dreams, and the ranch itself, survived.

"What are you worrying about?"

She glanced across at Camp and realized that, while he had his seat belt on, he hadn't yet started the truck. "Worrying?"

"That crease is back between your eyes."

"That's called age," she said wryly.

To her surprise, Camp reached over and smoothed the area between her brows with his thumb. The touch startled her and brought with it a warmth that was completely unexpected. "That," he said firmly, "is called worry."

Taking a deep breath, she exhaled slowly. "A little. Yes."

Avery thought Camp would question her more, but he started the engine and turned his attention to driving.

As they left her ranch and turned onto the main road, she forced her shoulders to relax. Even if this did turn out to be nothing more than a further opportunity for him to grill her for information, she wouldn't let herself be disappointed. She would view it as another step forward in his decision-making. She wanted desperately for that decision to be favorable. It wouldn't stop her if that wasn't the case. She'd find a way to help the wounded heroes who needed it, who needed the solace and comfort and, yes, the healing that horses and riding could bring them.

"It's back." Camp's quick glance her way held amusement.

"What? What's back?"

"That furrow."

This time she chuckled, and it surprised her that she could. "Busted. But at least I quit biting my nails."

"You bit your nails?"

"You sound surprised."

"I am, to be honest. I've always attributed that trait to insecurity. You're one of the strongest, most secure women I've ever encountered."

She didn't know what to say to that so she skirted what sounded like a true compliment. "I started biting my nails a couple of years ago, when I was letting Eddie make me feel crazy. I quit when I filed for a divorce."

"Interesting choice of words—that you 'let' him make you feel crazy."

For a moment, she didn't answer because she didn't

want to get deep into her marriage, into the things that Eddie had done, and the despair to which she'd nearly succumbed. Choosing her words carefully to steer past those times and those feelings she didn't want to ever experience again, she finally answered. "Some things, even some feelings, are a choice. It's that simple. I'll never again let another person have that much influence over me. Emotions are one thing. I may get hurt again. I'll surely have times I feel sad or disappointed, as well as happy and triumphant, but I'll never doubt myself again. I'll never let anyone do that to me. That's a choice."

"Good for you," Camp said softly.

* * *

At Avery's request, they made a brief stop at the sheriff's office. Camp liked the man, liked what his initial investigation into the town had told him about Farley. Honesty and integrity in law enforcement wasn't a rarity, but it was nothing to take for granted either.

Farley was clearly disappointed that he still couldn't offer anything concrete. "I promise I won't stop digging, but I can't say I expect to find who fired those shots, Avery. I'd be lying if I told you I did."

Silently, Camp agreed. There was about as much chance of that as finding the proverbial needle in a haystack.

"Did the garage get your SUV ready to go yet? I didn't check with them this morning, but Jeff told me they were close to being finished yesterday."

"No," Avery told him. "They called me earlier. The seat that was shipped to them from New Orleans came in minutes before closing yesterday evening, and it wasn't the right model. They're waiting for the replacement. Once that's delivered and installed, I can pick it up."

"Well, if you need one of us to run out to the ranch and get you when it's ready, just give me a call."

Avery's smile was affectionate, and Camp realized he didn't like seeing quite that much warmth toward the sheriff who seemed more than a little fond of her.

"I'm sure that won't be necessary, but I'll keep it in mind." She hesitated. "You haven't heard anything more about the *high flyers* you mentioned last time I was here?"

Camp suspected she would've worded that question much less vaguely if he hadn't been there. He knew she didn't trust him completely, and he couldn't blame her for that. She had to feel that anything he knew and heard could be used to deny her application. What she didn't realize was that not being approved for the program would be the least of her problems at that point.

"Nothing. I haven't heard a word." The sheriff didn't seem too happy about it either. "Nothing else has happened at your place, has it?"

"Nothing else? Other than dead animals in water troughs, and a saddle damaged with intent to get someone hurt, maybe even killed, and Marla being knocked down by someone trying to steal a yearling, you mean?"

Farley scrubbed his hand over his brow. "I'd lock him up if I could, Avery."

Her expression softened. "I know that, Ben. I don't fault you for any of this. I just don't know what to do about it."

"All you need to do is keep watching out for yourself, and I'll keep sending a patrol car through as often as I can."

But Camp could tell neither the sheriff nor Avery

believed, any more than he did, that those measures would be a deterrent to whoever was behind what was happening. At this point, he suspected that not even locking Eddie Danson up as the sheriff wanted to do would alter what had been set in motion.

Camp waited until they'd finished a meal that was well-prepared and all the more enjoyable for the company he was keeping before he said the things he knew would return that furrow between Avery's brows and maybe even tempt her to bite her nails again. He might have waited even longer, but his thoughts were too close to the surface, as close to the surface as his growing feelings for the woman across from him.

"You're staring at me," she told him.

"You're beautiful." And that was the absolute truth.

"It's not that kind of a stare."

"Busted," he tossed her own word back to her, "but you are beautiful."

Faint color touched her cheeks, and the look was good on her, but she was as strong as he'd told her she was and not to be distracted. "Let's go back to the *busted* part. What is it you're *not* saying?"

"I've started an investigation into your ex's activities."

"Why?" she asked clearly dismayed. "I told you he has nothing to do with New Hope any more. The property, the horses, everything is one hundred percent mine and what I want to do, what I *will* do, for the veterans has nothing to do with *him*."

"But he's put you, and the horses, at risk."

"That's my battle."

Not alone, he wanted to tell her. He was smart enough to refrain.

"All *you* need to do," she persisted, "is determine if I'm solvent—which I am—and whether I'm capable of meeting the needs of wounded veterans—which I am. If you can't see that by now, I don't think there's anything left I can show you to prove it. That frustrates me."

"I've seen enough to know that." He felt a pang at the way her face lit at the words.

"So, you'll approve New Hope for the program?"

He was glad they had finished eating, because he knew she wouldn't have kept her appetite with what he was going to tell her next.

"There's a problem."

Her shoulders dropped ever so slightly, but he saw it, saw the brief flash of happiness in her eyes fade.

"Okay." That one word was all she said, but her expression said volumes more.

"You were approved for the VA's equine therapy program nearly a year ago," Camp admitted.

Avery stared at Camp, her expression one of total disbelief. "That can't be. I've been waiting forever to hear back on my application."

"During the past year, monthly checks have been sent, signed, and cashed for daily therapy at your facility for four different veterans who don't exist."

"You're not making any sense."

But Camp saw a flash of some hidden something in those beautiful eyes that suddenly made him doubt, made him wonder if his attraction to her had caused him to make a mistake. But he'd started on this path, and even if it led to a place he didn't want to go, he had no choice but to continue the discussion.

"The person on our end has been terminated and

charged with fraud."

"And on this end?" She was watching him steadily, with that same unreadability he'd seen in her the first time they'd talked, the first time they'd shared a meal. And, he realized, that had only been a few days ago. Despite his feelings for her, he forced himself to remember that he'd known her barely a week. The fact that he'd researched her, dug into every facet of her life for several long weeks didn't make for knowing a person.

"That's why I'm here."

"Well," she said and, although her tone remained calm and even, he could hear the underlying bitterness, "I'm sure you've plundered through all the dirty laundry of my life with Eddie. You'll know those checks didn't come to me, haven't been deposited to the ranch account or my personal account."

Spine straight, she placed her crumpled linen napkin on the table. "I'd like to go back to the ranch now."

Still wondering if his emotions had control of his good sense, Camp reached across and took her hand to keep her from getting out of her chair. His orders were to keep the details of their investigation from her, but if she were guilty, she already knew them. If she wasn't, if she was the victim of her ex's guilt, his investigation had turned an unexpected corner. "The funds were mailed to a post office box in Alexander City, made out to you, signed with your signature. After our guy was identified, that post office box was closed."

Every bit of color drained from her face. "You're crazy or you're lying."

"You know I'm not. I wouldn't say it if I couldn't prove it."

She snatched her hand away and got to her feet. "One thing you can't prove is that I signed those checks because that never happened. I'll get my own ride back to the ranch. I don't want to talk to you or be around you, not right now."

Camp watched as she exited the restaurant with a quiet dignity that pulled at him, made him regret having been the one to tell her why he was really there, regret having hurt her. One thing he didn't regret was being the one sent to investigate her. He might later, if she were guilty as his superiors were convinced, but if not, he was going to be the one to prove her innocence.

He supposed she'd go straight to Sheriff Farley to get that ride back to the ranch, but he didn't take any chances with her safety. He paid the check quickly and followed her. From across the street, he watched as she and Farley exited the sheriff's office together before he got back in his truck and trailed them back to the ranch.

Chapter 11

Avery felt as if she'd been slapped. She'd walked the few blocks back to Ben Farley's office without even noticing her surroundings. She was grateful the sheriff hadn't asked a single question when she stepped back into his office and asked if one of his deputies could take her home. He'd given her a look, picked up his western style hat, and walked her out to his patrol car.

Ben remained mercifully uninquisitive, commenting upon the opening of the new barbershop in town, the weather, anything except what had caused her to leave Camp alone someplace in town and find her own way home. He pulled to a stop in front of her house and got out with her. Shooting a warning glance at the truck and driver that had followed them back, Ben gave her a hug.

"Do you want me to run him out of here?"

Avery followed the direction of his gaze to Camp's truck. She hadn't been aware that he'd been that close behind them, but she couldn't have said she was surprised by the fact either.

"It isn't that easy. He's government and he hasn't done anything wrong—at least not according to the law."

"Makes me no mind, Avery. You want him gone, he'll be gone." Ben smiled faintly, but his eyes held a glint of steel. "I like him well enough, but you've got a place in my heart and always will."

"Same here, Ben," she said huskily. "I'll be okay. Thanks for getting me home."

"If you need me, call me. I'll always come. You know that."

"I do know."

She watched as the sheriff got back in his car and pulled away. He stopped briefly and put his window down to say something to Camp. She couldn't hear and didn't care. The feeling of numbed disbelief had given way to a burning anger. And it didn't help that the anger was directed more at herself than anyone else. Camp, it seemed, was just doing his job. If she was a casualty, well, business was business.

Although she could feel his gaze on her as she walked back into her house to change, she was careful not to even glance at him. So much for feeling attractive, for *being attracted*. She had a ranch to run. Sooner or later, she and Camp would have to talk again, she knew. She was under investigation and if she ran him off, the government would send someone else.

The government. Realization hummed through her veins. That she was under scrutiny of federal authorities scared her. It was one thing to be judged fit or unfit to be part of a VA program. Being judged guilty or not guilty, subject to being charged with fraud against the federal government, was another thing entirely. A truly frightening thing.

The whole time she changed back into jeans and tee shirt, her mind spun with the implications. She knew she was innocent. Still, if Camp was right in everything he said—and there was very little possibility he wasn't—it meant someone had forged her name and taken money intended to help wounded veterans, maybe even set her up to take this fall.

That last thought had her pausing as she unpinned her hair and pulled it through the back of her ball cap.

That someone had to be Eddie but her mind reeled to think he'd been either that desperate or that determined to destroy her. But if Eddie had meant to set her up for jail and take control of the ranch, why hadn't he? Cold feet? Or was it only and ever the money? Only and ever his gambling debts driving him? And how could she prove his guilt and clear herself?

Sighing, Avery pulled on her socks and boots. Camp had made it clear that he believed she was the guilty party. Or had he? She got to her feet, and then stood, thinking. Camp hadn't said *signed by you*. He'd said *signed with your signature*. She wasn't sure if there was a difference in his mind. He hadn't hinted at any belief in her innocence, just stated the bare facts and rather baldly at that. Even if there was a difference in his mind, the difference would be in whether or not she went to federal prison for something she hadn't done. It wouldn't change that she had almost trusted him, almost let herself feel something for him.

Never again. She'd trust herself, her horses, and the team that had proven their loyalty to her over and over again.

The thought of prison terrified her. The thought of what would happen to her horses in that eventuality brought a cold clamminess to her skin. She had to force herself to breathe against the weight that pressed down on her. No, she wasn't going there again, either. She wasn't, wouldn't be helpless. She'd already proven she was a fighter, and she'd fight this with her last ounce of strength and willpower. She would *not* be a victim, not to Eddie or anyone else.

A low-throated rumble had her glancing down. "Callahan, hey." Bending down to stroke him, she took comfort from the warmth of his body, the feel of his soft coat against her fingers. She still wasn't sure why he'd pushed his way into her life, and he might be here for only a little while, but she'd enjoy him while he was.

Marla stepped into the kitchen from the garden door as Avery walked through from the hall. "Hi," Marla said, studying her closely. "I was checking on you."

"I'm fine." Avery did her best to smile. "Any reason I wouldn't be?"

Marla gave a laugh that didn't sound the least bit happy. "It never seems to end, does it?"

"Has something else happened?" Avery felt her heart clutch.

"No, thank God. I'm feeling edgy, I guess."

Marla was normally such an undemonstrative person that it caught Avery off guard when she stepped closer and leaned her head against Avery's shoulder. She gave her stepdaughter a light hug and was neither surprised nor offended when Marla moved away again almost at once. Eddie had told her once that, after Missy's death,

Marla's mother had ceased to show any sign of affection to either her husband or her remaining daughter. Marla had withdrawn more and more, and it was still rare for her to initiate touching any human, though she was openly affectionate with the horses, and Avery had long suspected she had some feelings for Tucker that she was careful to hide when he was watching.

"Jake Everett is supposed to be here in about half an hour. Hopefully I'll find out why he's dragging his feet over the fenced riding path."

The project she'd mentioned to Camp, but never had the chance to elaborate on, was a safe place she'd designed for sightless clients to ride with some sense of independence. When finished, it would be a riding path with tall, sturdy fencing, lined on the inside with soft-leaved shrubs. It would be a means for those without sight but who wanted a sense of independence, like Sergeant Gallagher, to ride in safety. If they inadvertently guided their mount too close to the fence, their knees would hit a living hedge rather than unyielding posts and boards. When finished, the route would wind over a full five acres of level ground. With a raised platform, she, or one of her team, would be able to see the rider at all times and reach him—or her—within minutes if need be.

"I'll go with you to meet him," Marla said.

"Well, you're always welcome, but I can deal with whatever is keeping Mr. Everett from completing his work here. If I have to, I'll fire him and find someone else to finish the job. I don't care if it *is* mid-stream of the project."

"I'm going." Marla was adamant. "He might not take kindly to being fired."

Avery shook her head in exasperation. "Marla, I'll be

fine. Again, you're welcome but there's no need."

Marla ignored that. "We can take the ranch truck." She hesitated. "Maybe later we can go for a ride. Just us."

And that was when Avery got it, saw the uncertainty, the hint of insecurity. Marla had clung to her side when she and Eddie first married, transitioned to a poised young adult in the years after, but returned to a more fragile state as Eddie had slowly deteriorated, destroying Avery's trust and their marriage. Marla would never cling, but it was clear she needed to be close to Avery for now.

"A ride sounds wonderful, Marla." Avery didn't have to pretend her pleasure at the thought. It would be good to get away, enjoy the horses as the afternoon faded and the blistering heat eased.

Marla nodded. "Good. Now let's go tackle Mr. Everett. Figuratively, that is," she added with a grin.

* * *

Jake Everett stepped out of his truck as they approached. He leaned one hip against the hood and watched as they climbed down from the ranch truck and walked toward him. Behind him five acres of the flattest land on her ranch had been studded with tall, sturdy posts waiting for boards to be run at several different levels.

"Mr. Everett," Avery offered her hand and, though the man took it, she could both see and feel his reluctance to do so.

He was a lean man, weathered by the work he did in the sun and the wind, the heat, and the cold. His company had a solid reputation for delivering quality work on time. Avery knew because she'd vetted that company well and selected it, and him, with care. It had surprised her when he and his crew had stopped work halfway without so much as a word to her. She'd waited until the work was a month past due before contacting him, more because those final days of court had drained her than for any patience on her part. She'd paid half of the total up front, trusting that Jake Everett would live up to his promise. What he'd done so far was quality work, but now she needed it finished.

Because the man didn't show any inclination to address the problem, Avery decided to take the bull by the horns. "I appreciate you coming out to talk with me. I would've appreciated more if you'd finished the job on time like you promised."

He flushed a dark red. "And I would've appreciated not being put in the position I'm in with the lumber yard."

Avery realized that what she'd taken for embarrassment was anger, pure and simple. "What do you mean?"

"Ma'am, half that material you ordered—and then had hauled away from the lumber store without paying—has nothing to do with what I'm doing out here for you. I've built a reputable company with hard, honest work. I don't want my name associated with anything less than honest dealings."

Avery felt a slow burn heat her from the inside out, but she could feel Marla bristling beside her and placed a hand on the girl's arm. "Mr. Everett, I don't know what you're accusing me of or what you're talking about. I've paid for everything that's been delivered, everything you've put in the ground and what's laying there stacked, ready to be put up. Like I paid you up front, believing you'd do a good job."

"And that's what I've done. A good job. And I'll finish

once you're square with the lumber yard, and I can look Stu Sykes in the eye again."

"Who?" Avery stared at him in complete bewilderment. "Who is Stu Sykes?"

"Owns a lumber yard a few miles north of town."

Marla wasn't being silent. She shook off Avery's hand and stepped forward with a fierce glare. "I don't know Stu Sykes, and I've never placed an order with that lumber yard. That is *not* where we got the posts *or* any of the rest of the material. We got everything here in town, local. Like we buy everything else. *Local.* I paid for it myself and watched it being unloaded."

Jake Everett rubbed the back of his neck as he looked from one to the other. Clearly, being on the receiving end of a female's wrath wasn't his idea of a good time. He focused on Avery. "If you buy everything local, why'd your husband call and ask me where to get the best deal? Hell, I even told Stu he could let the man send someone to pick it up—that I didn't have a doubt in the world you'd put the check in the mail that same day like he promised."

Before Avery could even open her mouth, Marla said the dirtiest word Avery had ever heard her utter.

"I'll pay Mr. Sykes tomorrow. From my own account. You finish this job as you promised, and you'll get paid the second half of the money as you were promised." Marla swung on her heels, then swung back. "I'll tell you one thing, Mr. Everett, you're no more a man than my dad. A real man wouldn't have walked away from a commitment without a word of explanation. A real man would've had the brass to come speak his mind up front instead of waiting for his client to call and ask what the hell was going on. Avery is the most honest person you'll ever meet. She pays every bill *before* it even comes due. Ask anyone in town. You and your Mr. Sykes are dumb as dirt to take the word of a jerk you don't even know, over the phone, and hand him thousands of dollars worth of material."

Marla stalked away, leaving Avery to stare after her a moment. She glanced back at Jake Everett and almost apologized before deciding Marla was right. He *hadn't* been man enough to call her and give her a chance to explain or deny. "If you plan to finish the job, be here first thing tomorrow and every day after until it's done. The first day I don't see you and you don't call and say why, I give the job to someone else, and they get the rest of the money."

Marla was crying without making a sound when Avery reached the truck and climbed behind the wheel. "I'm sorry."

"Marla, you have nothing to apologize for, and no, you won't pay this Mr. Sykes. I'm going to take the man a copy of the notice my attorney put in the paper when I was granted a legal separation. He can go after Eddie for the money if he wants to. Neither you nor I are responsible. And if I never see another man, it will be too soon," she smiled a little and added, "except Tucker." Then she started the engine and put the truck in drive. "Now let's go saddle up."

All of the things Avery wouldn't say to Marla were spinning through her mind as she drove back toward the barns. What Eddie had done made no sense. What on earth would he do with posts and lumber? He could have absolutely no use for fence material.

As if reading her mind, Marla said. "He sold it. Probably had someone—whoever picked it up—ready and willing to pay a fraction of what it's worth. Quick cash. Damn it!"

Marla's clenched fist pounded her thigh and she repeated with even more emphasis, "*Damn* it!"

Avery gave her stepdaughter a quick glance and sighed at the expression on her face.

"You don't own this, Marla, and neither do I."

"He's my dad."

"And I was his wife. Doesn't make us responsible."

Marla smiled ever so slightly. "Doesn't make us *dumb as dirt,* as Misters Sykes and Everett either."

"Exactly right. Now let's give all of this a rest and enjoy what's left of our day, okay?"

The tension in Marla's shoulders eased visibly. "Yeah. Let's."

* * *

I'm not real keen on the fact that Avery and Marla are out alone, and it's clear as glass that Camp isn't any happier about it than I am. He watched with a scowl as they rode out on some singularly large horses. They're not two of the livelier ones, it's true, just large. In fact, the one Avery calls Jack, the one she saddled, is a gentle creature, but still they've been gone some time now, and Camp is almost making me edgy with his stalking about as he watches the horizon for their return. And I'm not the nervous sort.

The sun is getting low along the horizon and while the clouds are a nice crimson as if lit from within, that sunset isn't what's holding Camp's attention any more than it is mine.

And while I've heard a coyote or two and even a wild cat of some sort, it's not four-legged creatures that concern me. There's evil out there. I did note a shotgun secured into the leather scabbard on Marla's saddle and she may be as excellent a shot as she is an equestrian or she wouldn't bother with a weapon, but that's a small consolation. I have to wonder if she could shoot anyone, much less her own father if he proves to be the one behind Avery's ongoing misfortune. And, for my part, it's almost a sure bet that he is.

Based on his behavior on the courthouse steps, I don't think he poses any physical threat, not face to face. He crumbled like pie crust when confronted. He's a coward, and either of the ladies could bring him down if forced to it. No, the real threat is going to be from men he's made very, very angry. That's my opinion, and I'm rarely wrong.

At last, they're making their way down the hill closest to the paddock area. And not a moment too soon, as the sun is slipping farther and farther and the shadows are deepening. Horses may have vision equal to mine, but I'd rather not have Avery's safety hanging on a possibility.

* * *

"Callahan, that's one hard-headed woman." Camp propped a foot on the lower rung of a paddock and watched as Avery and Marla rode into the barn and began the task of unsaddling and grooming.

Marla had acknowledged his presence with a quiet greeting as they'd passed by him. Avery had simply given him a cool glance, which had Marla studying her curiously.

Camp bided his time until they were finished with their mounts, then gave a hand as they, with Leanne and Tucker, fed and hayed the horses. Whether that helping hand was wanted or not, he couldn't have said and didn't much care. If Avery had said anything to the others about their conversation at lunch, he couldn't tell. The three of them acted the same as they always had, comfortable in his presence, accepting he was there and not likely to go away until his investigation was finished. Only Avery continued to give him a chilly shoulder. She wasn't blatant about it. But he knew.

When everything was done that needed to be, he fell into step beside her as she walked back to her house. Marla had stayed behind, talking with Tucker about one of the two-year-olds he thought might be ready for some additional handling. Camp had learned that all of the youngsters knew how to be led and would allow themselves to be brushed and combed by the time they were two-year-olds and that none would be ridden until they were three but it seemed there was plenty for them to learn in between the leading and the riding.

Avery didn't acknowledge his presence. Camp didn't bother to speak. He didn't need to remind her that he strode close at her side. She knew perfectly well he was there.

It wasn't until they reached the door that she stopped and turned back to him. "Go away."

"You're putting off a conversation that's going to be had."

"It's not going to be had tonight. I'm tired and I'm not going to talk to you now, so go away."

Camp sighed. "I'm not the bad guy, Avery."

"You're not the good guy, either." It was a stark reminder of his purpose in her life.

Camp didn't try to stop her as she went inside and closed the door firmly behind her. "Damn it," he said softly. He turned to go and nearly stumbled over Callahan, who was sitting at his feet, staring up at him with what seemed to be an accusatory expression.

Camp gave a grunt and stepped around him. Tomorrow, Avery would have to talk with him. The problem was Camp didn't have a clue what he was going to say to her.

Chapter 12

Avery woke feeling heavy-lidded and weighted down. Somewhere in her dreams the peace of mind she'd gained by the simple act of riding with Marla along the slopes and ridges of the valley had slipped away. She'd been invigorated by their discussion of future plans for the ranch and possible expansions of existing programs. Unfortunately, Avery could no longer put aside the reality that she was being investigated for fraud by the government. It was a reality she hadn't shared with Marla. In one sense, they were truly partners, but in another they would always have that mother-daughter relationship. Avery didn't see any need to distress Marla more than she already was, just as she suspected Marla had shielded Avery from some of the uglier things her father had said over the course of their separation and divorce.

Sighing at the inevitable, she dressed and found her boots. She'd send Camp the usual text about coffee and breakfast, but if he stayed more than another day or two, she planned to purchase a coffee pot and cookware for his bungalow. She wished she'd done that already because she definitely did not feel like facing whatever he felt he needed to say to her. On a whim, she grabbed her own coffee before she hit send and headed out to the barn. It was an evasion tactic but she felt entitled, all things considered.

The air had that slight morning coolness, which she knew would dissipate as soon as the sun hit the tree line. Still, she enjoyed it while she could, settling in one of the canvas chairs they kept throughout the barns for such moments as this, at the beginning or end of a busy day. Jack thrust his head over the stall door and nickered at her as she stretched her legs and crossed them at the ankles in front of her.

"Good morning to you, too," she said softly.

As he nickered again, more urgently, she chuckled. "I'm going to finish this cup of coffee then check the chalkboard, but I suspect you've all been fed."

"You're right, he has," Leanne said, stepping around the corner, "but that won't stop him from begging."

Some horses would quit eating when they were full, some would eat and then eat again if they could and, like the consequences of the wrong feed or poor-quality feed, overfeeding could be devastating. Colic or founder too often ended in death. Founder could leave a horse crippled and in a lifetime of pain. Those risks were why her crew was extremely careful to check and double-check on feeding before covering someone else's barn.

And Jack was in Leanne's barn because he, of all of the horses, had the strongest affinity for those wounded in mind as well as body. That characteristic, passed down to his offspring, was a large part of what had made New Hope Ranch successful in the art and practice of equine therapy. And that was where Avery's heart had turned, and she knew it was where it would remain. She could have made a comfortably good living providing nothing but riding lessons for youngsters, but that first foster child, abused physically and mentally, had set her and Jack on a different course.

It had taken time to build their clientele, to vet riding instructors with other facilities, until she could successfully and confidently accept the referrals of those happy, healthy children and adults who wanted the opportunity to learn to ride. Now, so many physicians and counselors referred patients to her, she couldn't take all of them without another barn filled with horses that were suited to the task. Someday, hopefully soon, she'd have that. Meanwhile, she managed to find a way to take the ones that seemed to need her most, conferring with the referring professional, reading through summaries of treatment released to her by the patient or their primary caregiver.

Avery looked up from her reverie to find Leanne still standing and watching her. She tilted her head in silent question.

"You don't look like you slept well," Leanne said bluntly.

"I know." No point in denying the fact. She'd seen for herself the shadows under her eyes as she'd combed her hair and pulled it through a ball cap.

"Anything I can do to help?"

"Shoot me."

"Well, now *that* would solve everything." Leanne's tone was dry.

Avery chuckled. "Sorry. Just tired of dealing with the mess I made of my life. But I'm off my pity pot. I've got a couple of clients this morning, but there's something I need to take care of later. I'll let you know when I head out."

"Do you need me or Tuck to go with you?"

Leanne had asked the question with studied carelessness but she appeared troubled, and Avery realized it was a look she was seeing too often.

"No, just a paperwork issue I've got to take care of."

"Something you're not letting Marla handle?"

Avery realized her light explanation had done nothing to erase Leanne's anxious expression. Paperwork was Marla's venue, and they all knew it.

"Marla's got a full plate. It's end of month closeout, and she mentioned a trip into town to pick up a few bales of alfalfa until our shipment arrives. Besides, the worst of this trip is the drive time out to a lumber business some miles north of town." That was pretty much a flat-out lie, but Avery considered it a necessary one. There was no danger in what she was doing or where she was going, just an unpleasantness that was hers, not Marla's, to manage.

Leanne didn't look entirely convinced but she nodded and turned to go. After a few steps, she glanced back over her shoulder at Avery, her expression almost fierce in its intensity. "And you didn't make a mess of your life, Avery. You fell in love, and you trusted a man who wasn't deserving of either your love or your trust but that's on him—not you."

Avery watched Leanne stride away and sighed. She appreciated the sentiment but suspected she should have been wise enough to discern that Eddie wasn't the man she thought him to be at the start. Clearly, her judgement hadn't been what it should have, not then and—apparently—not now. Her attraction to Camp was ill-advised to say the least. A man who would dig until he decided whether or not she was guilty and too bad if the verdict wasn't a good one for her. Nope, her judgement wasn't to be trusted at all, not where men were concerned.

"At least not human males, right, Jack?" She rose to scratch lightly behind his ears then walked out into the heat of the morning. It was time to start her day. She returned to the house, ready to deal with Camp once and for all, but judging by the nearly full pot, he'd chosen to ignore her routine offer of coffee and the use of her kitchen. Wise man.

* * *

Camp had decided to steer clear of Avery though the ping as her text came through tugged at him on a visceral level. Reluctantly, he'd set the phone aside without answering. A trail bar and bottle of water would have to suffice. Avery needed a cooling off period. He did, too, but not for the same reasons. He'd been on his laptop half the night, digging deeper and deeper into the past and present of Eddie Danson, and he'd resumed that search long before getting Avery's text.

Her ex was a piece of work, for sure. On the surface, he was a man in debt up to his eyeballs with all the typical trappings of that status. Gas card limit maxed out, hefty credit card balances for the most expensive men's clothing and liquor stores, a bank note he had no apparent means of paying for the exact amount of the deposit he'd made on a ritzy apartment the day after Avery's divorce was granted.

Below the surface was an uglier story. Avery had mentioned *high flyer* when talking with Farley the day before. It wasn't all that difficult for Camp to delve into the local casino's financial records. What he found made him wince. Eddie liked to play blackjack for some pretty high stakes, and he didn't win very often. But Camp knew perfectly well that what was recorded was the tip of an iceberg laden with 'chips across the table' depths. The casino seemed legit in their record-keeping, but there were ways for less than honest players to keep cash exchanges out of sight and off the record.

Camp hadn't had much reason to investigate gamblers before, but he knew someone who would have. He noted a couple of the names involved and shot off a quick e-mail to Trey Hyatt before collecting his truck keys, sunglasses, and cap from the small table that stood near the door. He made the trip into town at a casual speed, his thoughts divided between the road ahead, his investigation, and his feelings for Avery. Heading straight to one end of the tree-lined street in front of the courthouse, he stepped out of the truck knowing that his boots and jeans were sufficiently worn that he wouldn't stand out from any other citizen with business in town.

He didn't expect to have any new insight, but his gaze scanned both sides of the street as he walked. There were numerous places a man could have waited in the dusk and taken an easy shot, before disappearing without notice.

Camp reached the spot where Avery's truck had been

parked but walked past without hesitating. There was nothing to see there now, and his morning stroll hadn't revealed anything that he didn't already know.

The diner he'd spotted on his initial trip into town was bustling as he stepped inside. Noting the sign, which had been turned from *Please Wait to Be Seated* to *Please Take a Seat*, he made his way to a booth near the back.

A waitress with neatly pinned hair slid him a one-page laminated menu. "Good morning. What can I get you to drink?"

"Coffee, please."

"Do you know what you want or do you need a few minutes?"

Camp flipped the menu over from the lunch selections to the breakfast items on the back. "You can add a BLT to that coffee."

"You got it," she said with a quick smile as he handed the menu back to her.

The coffee was strong, the bacon crispy, and the waitress wasn't nosey, so Camp enjoyed the meal. He was on his second cup of coffee when his phone alerted him of incoming mail. It was a two-lined response from Trey to his earlier query. "At a glance, these are not people you want to take out to dinner. File to follow later. Still digging."

With a sigh, Camp finished his coffee, paid his bill, and retrieved his cap from the bench beside him. He'd watch for the file, but he didn't need it to know Danson had brought a pile of bad down on everyone around him. Still leaving his truck where he'd parked it, he walked the short distance to the sheriff's office. Farley was stepping out onto the sidewalk and stopped when he saw Camp. He pushed his hat back a little further on his head and acknowledged Camp with an unsmiling nod.

Camp felt sure the sheriff wasn't a fan of his after whatever Avery had told him yesterday, but he didn't much care and didn't bother with niceties. "Are you keeping an eye on Danson?"

"I pretty much keep an eye on everything and everyone in my town." Farley's tone was mild, a lot milder than the hard gleam in his eyes.

"Well, someone sure seems to be getting by you on their way to Avery's place pretty often."

Farley rubbed the back of his neck and looked down at the sidewalk a minute before looking back at Camp. "Kirkland, if you want a fight, I can give you one, but I don't think it will help anything that's going on out there. I'm madder at myself than you are about that and, if I had to guess, I'd say it's about the same with you."

Camp took a deep breath and let the tension slide from his shoulders. "Yeah. I want to take a punch at somebody right now, but I reckon it's not you. I've got a friend taking a hard look at the men Danson's been mixing with at the casino. I'd like to hear what you know."

"It may not be enough to help, but I'm willing to share if you've got time to take a walk."

Camp fell into step with the sheriff and asked, "How long have you known Eddie Danson?"

"Just since he married Avery. He seemed like an okay guy for a long time, not a go-getter, mind you, but decent. He set up office as a financial adviser for a while here in town, but I don't think trade was real brisk. He closed the place after the first year's lease was up, and Avery said he was working from the ranch. Guess that's a business you can keep pretty much online. Must have been fairly successful, though.'"

"Based on…?"

"Drove some pretty sporty cars over the years and sent Marla to a very good university. And Avery's way too smart to take care of a man who can't take care of himself."

"You don't think he bought those cars with the ranch money he was helping himself
to?"

"Avery told you about that, did she?" Farley shot him a sideways glance before adding, "No, that came later. I'll admit I did some digging when I started hearing rumors about his gambling. Not from Avery, mind you. She's one to keep things to herself until she can't. He was making money, at least for a while."

"These guys Danson gambled with and owes money to—any of them local?"

"No, best I can tell they're from up around Birmingham. Fly in and out on a chartered plane. Pretty much always come in together. Don't frequent the women. Don't drink. Just gamble and leave."

"Any indication of cheating?"

"Not that I know … and I would. I golf with the manager there on a regular basis."

Camp mulled that over, making sure he didn't have any other questions that the sheriff could answer for him. Their conversation, which they'd kept in low tones, had been interrupted frequently by residents greeting their sheriff and giving Camp the once-over. They'd walked through most of the town streets and would soon be fairly close to where Camp had parked his truck.

"I guess Marla's running errands."

Camp looked up and followed the sheriff's glance

across the street where she was stepping out of an office supply store. She met their gazes and strode across the street toward them. She nodded at Camp and smiled at Farley.

"Hey, Ben. Things okay with you?"

"Fine, Marla, how about yourself?"

"I'm good. I checked with the garage and Avery's SUV is almost ready to go, said for sure by six o'clock closing. I'm going to leave my car parked beside the library in a little while. Don't tow it off, okay?"

The sheriff chuckled and shook his head. "It'd be safe from me, but why don't you let me have a deputy run the SUV out there on their next round your way?"

"Well …" Marla chuckled, admitting, "I've got my eye on a few things in town that won't fit in my trunk."

"Okay, give me your key and I'll make sure your car gets home safe."

"I'll take you up on that, but I'll bring the key and the car around to your office later. Got some places left to go first. And I appreciate you keeping a watch on the ranch and Avery."

"On you, too, Marla," the sheriff reminded. "And that won't ease up until things settle down."

Marla took her leave, acknowledging Camp with another nod. He suspected she was as unhappy with him as Avery was.

As she walked away, Camp commented, "She and Avery are close."

"They are that. I suspect Marla would fight tigers for Avery. Her father's behavior can't be anything but an embarrassment to her."

Camp took his leave of the sheriff, knowing he'd

learned all he was going to and knowing, too, that nothing he'd heard was going to be of much help, just as the sheriff had said. Time to head back to the ranch and check to see if Trey had finished his digging.

Time, too, to have that conversation with Avery, the one she'd been avoiding.

* * *

Avery parked the ranch truck in front of Sykes Lumber Yard and put the windows down. As she turned the engine off, Callahan stood and stretched. "I can't imagine why you insisted on coming with me," Avery commented. "I've never in my life known a cat that liked to ride in a vehicle."

But then, she had to admit, she'd never known a cat quite like Callahan. Taking a deep breath, she opened the door and slid from the truck seat. She pulled the photocopy she'd made of her attorney's newspaper notice from her purse then realized she couldn't leave her purse in the truck, not with the windows down. And she couldn't put them up and lock the doors with Callahan inside. Not in this heat.

"You're a lot of trouble," she said.

Callahan merely observed her through eyes narrowed against the glare of the late afternoon sun. The drive had taken her longer than expected. Her GPS hadn't accounted for the poor condition of the roads.

Slinging her purse straps over one shoulder, she stuffed the paper back inside, closed the truck door, and walked to the front entrance. The cavernous room she entered appeared to be part office and part showroom with samples of hardwood and natural stone countertop displayed. Apparently, Sykes believed in diversifying his business enterprise. There were three different desks but none of the leather chairs were occupied.

"Hello?"

Silence answered so she crossed to the wide doorway at the back of the showroom and found herself in a warehouse of sorts. Following the sound of voices, she made her way to the other end where two men in jeans and a woman in leggings and a long, sleeveless shirt watched as a semi was being loaded with lumber.

They didn't seem to have heard her footsteps above the sound of the forklift so she lifted her voice a little and said, "Mr. Sykes?"

The thinner, older man turned toward her. "Yes, ma'am, I'm Mr. Sykes. Can I help you with something? I'm sorry none of us were up front. Excuse me a minute." He turned from her to the woman. "Sharon, you need to get back to your work area."

The woman—actually more like girl, Avery realized as she turned around—rolled her eyes at him but did as she was told. She shot Avery a grin that said the girl didn't hold her responsible for being sent back to work.

Sykes turned his attention back to Avery. "Now, ma'am, what can I do for you?"

"I'm Avery Wilson—previously Avery Danson."

And that quick, his demeanor changed from helpful to borderline hostile. "You brought my check?"

The younger man turned around at the words, and Avery could see the family resemblance between them.

"No, I'm afraid I don't owe you anything."

"Now see here," he stepped closer. "Your husband sent a truck out here to pick up several thousand dollars' worth of my lumber."

Avery stood her ground. "Ex-husband."

"Not at the time, he wasn't!" His face took on a dark red tone.

She handed him the photocopy she'd brought. "You'll want to read this."

He read it and glared at her. "Won't stand up in court."

"Yes, sir, it will. I have an excellent attorney."

"I'll make you and him sorry," he threatened.

The sound of a warning yowl echoed eerily through the warehouse.

"What the hell was that!"

Avery sighed as a second yowl, closer, bounced off the walls. "That would be Callahan."

She watched as the gray cat made his way closer. His back was arched, and his hair bristled.

"Well, get him out of here. The next time you see me will be in court."

"I'm confident I won't ever see you again, Mr. Sykes, not once you show any attorney you engage that piece of paper. They won't waste *their* time, even if you want to waste *yours*."

With an air of calm she didn't feel, Avery turned and retraced her steps through the business, the cat close at her heels. Her knees were trembling, but she was careful not to show it. Not for the world would she let the man take it for fear, instead of the anger it was.

Chapter 13

Camp couldn't decide if he should feel irritated or reprieved when he returned to the ranch and Avery was nowhere to be found. What he did feel was a hum of tension, along with a thread of self-awareness because he recognized that tension reflected equal parts disappointment and concern. Nor did he fool himself that his concern for her safety was due to nothing more than the bone-deep military training that gave him a sense of responsibility for civilians in general.

Telling himself he was an idiot for being glad that one gray cat was missing as well—after all, how much protection could a cat provide—he settled in to read what Trey had sent. Superficially, there was nothing that would alarm the average reader. Eddie had been playing with a tight trio of independently-wealthy, high rollers. That appellation—independently wealthy—should have implied that winning or losing wouldn't necessarily be a big deal, right? It was all about the game. But Trey had dug deep. With growing misgivings, Camp read on through the misfortunes that had plagued a long line of fringe players like Avery's ex. Some had been *lucky* enough to win large amounts from them, others unlucky enough to lose sums they couldn't repay. Camp flipped through pages of newspaper photocopy, a drowning on a boating excursion in the Keys here, a hunting accident in Texas canyon country there, and even a suicide.

The report had been written in Trey's sparse style and, really, he didn't need to use many words. Trey knew Camp was more than capable of reading between the lines. Danson had put himself opposite some dangerous people. Himself and anyone associated with him.

Restless and mad as hell at a man too stupid to know what he'd done, Camp reached for his cap and strode out toward the paddocks.

Tucker was leading a horse back to the barn as a small car pulled out toward the open road beyond the ranch. Tucker greeted him with a smile that faded quickly. "You don't look happy."

"Understatement."

"Anything I need to know?"

Camp hesitated then shook his head. "Nothing you don't already. Danson's an asshole."

"No argument, there. After I put this fellow up, I'm headed out to check the progress on the enclosed riding path. The contractor finally showed back up to work. Want to tag along?"

Restless and, admittedly, curious, Camp nodded and

fell into step with Tucker as he headed for the truck.

As they bounced along what was little more than a cow path, Camp asked, "What, exactly, is an enclosed riding path?"

"Well," Tucker scratched his head, "to tell the truth, I don't know how to describe it. I don't have anything to compare it to. It's an Avery invention. She got the idea from Sergeant Gallagher who keeps pushing for her to let him ride outside the paddock."

"That's the young man who lost his vision overseas?"

"Yeah, an IED." Tucker's tone was grim. "Stinkin' shame."

"It always is," Camp agreed. "So young Gallagher wants to extend his boundaries."

"And Avery is determined to help him do that. She set aside five acres and hired one of the local contractors to enclose a walking trail. Took us several nights to lay out the design to make the best use of the acreage because she wanted it to be something that would give the rider a sense of open spaces, not just a bigger circle than the riding paddocks they're usually in when they ride. There couldn't be any angles to give a horse reason to stop, so it's all curves."

Tucker stopped the truck close to several large trees that Camp thought were some kind of oak but not the huge, live oak that covered so much of the South. The sun was large and red and almost riding the horizon. Before them were a half dozen or so tanned, leathered workmen in well-worn jeans and tee shirts and what seemed to him like a maze of fence posts, hundreds of them, with no particular pattern.

As they climbed out of the truck and walked closer, Camp could see the railing that was going up. Instead of three evenly spaced rows of railing similar to that around the riding paddocks, six boards were being fitted top to bottom in the middle of the span. And, instead of being placed on the outside of the posts for a nice, neat look, they were being nailed on the inside. Camp opened his mouth to ask about the oddity then realized the safety of the design. A rider without sight would not find his boot hung in an unexpected and potentially hazardous position against a fence post. Avery was taking no chances with the well-being of Gallagher, or any other sightless riders who placed their trust in her. She wasn't building for beauty but for safety.

Tucker shook hands with one of the men, greeting him by name, and slapping an arm lightly to his shoulder. "Camp, this is my cousin, once or twice removed. Hadley Small, Camp Kirkland."

Camp held out a hand and found the man had a grip that matched the muscles bulging from his forearm.

Hadley, it turned out, was foreman for the group. He glanced at his watch and called it a day. He walked back toward the trees with Tucker and Camp even as he kept an eye on his crew while they gathered up their tools and placed them in the job boxes attached to the work truck.

"I'm glad to see you and your men back at work here," Tucker said.

"Yeah," Hadley agreed, "me, too. Close to home for a change. What happened here, anyway? Jake pulled us off, out of the blue, and sent us to another job two counties over. I asked him more than once about coming back to finish but he wouldn't even talk with me about it."

"A misunderstanding," Tucker said, but his voice was grim.

Hadley nodded. "It happens," he said easily, "but I'm

glad we're going to finish what we started. I don't like leaving things undone. Besides, I like Ms. Avery and what she's got going on out here. I wish my sister, Jean, lived closer. Her second kid was diagnosed with cerebral palsy. She's got him in a good program where she is, one of the best, but I think this thing with the horses could help, too."

"Jean moved to New Orleans when she got married, didn't she? I'll ask Avery to check out some riding facilities in that area. She's got a bunch of contacts in about every state," Tucker offered. "I won't keep you from supper, Hadley. I wanted to make sure work had started again. Looks like y'all are making good progress, too."

"The railing won't take as long as the fence posts," Hadley assured him.

The two chatted a few minutes before Hadley rounded up his crew for the trip back to town. Tucker and Camp pulled out right behind the work truck.

As they rode back to the barn, Camp asked, "What was the misunderstanding?"

Tucker told him about Eddie's sleight of hand with the lumber while Camp listened in silence. "I expect that much material cost a pretty penny," was all he said.

"Close to eight thousand, according to Marla," Tucker agreed.

"Seems like a complicated ruse."

Tucker shot him a look. "Yep, but it worked."

Camp didn't answer. Apparently, it *had* worked but something felt off about the whole thing. There seemed a pretty big risk to Eddie of finding himself in some real legal trouble since he'd identified himself openly to the owner of the lumber yard. Camp didn't like the sense of growing desperation that implied.

Tucker stopped the truck in front of his barn, and Camp followed the younger man inside to help with the evening feed. He missed his gym time, though there was plenty to do around here to at least stretch his muscles, if not really work them. Morning and evening push-ups did that but he was getting bored with that routine and craved the equipment in his basement gym.

As they worked, Camp was increasingly aware of Avery's absence and the slowly gathering dark. He heard Leanne before Tucker did, probably because he was listening so hard for the sound of an engine to signal Avery's return.

"Tucker! Tucker, where are you?"

Before either could respond, Leanne ran breathlessly into the barn, her face filled with fear and fury. "Marla's hurt. She was bringing Avery's SUV back to the ranch and someone ran her off the road near the old Roberts' place. Deliberately—that was the word she used. The vehicle rolled, and she hit her head. She thinks she lost consciousness for a while but her voice was weak and I couldn't hear everything she was saying. Then she disconnected. I called for an ambulance, but now I can't get her back."

Camp's first thought iced the blood in his veins. Avery was somewhere along that same road.

Tucker wheeled to run and Camp grabbed his arm. "With me," he said, taking charge because that's what he did. And Tucker, looking shell-shocked and frantic, nodded.

Camp turned to Leanne. "Do you have a gun?"

"I do and I'm good with it. What the hell is going on?"

"I'm not sure, but keep whatever firearm you have on you and loaded until we get back. If Avery takes another route and misses Marla and us, keep her here, whatever it takes. Call the sheriff's office to send someone out here until I get back. Tucker and I will make sure Marla is safe." He wasn't sure if her startled glance had to do with the avalanche of orders, the fact that he thought a loaded gun was a necessity, or the familiarity with which he'd spoken of Avery. No 'Ms. Avery' or 'Ms. Wilson' now.

With Tucker giving directions, Camp drove with the speed and skill he'd learned in emergency training, navigating sharp curves as easily as straightaways. He didn't like the fact that the light was fading, partly due to the time and partly to the overhang of clouds. "How far is this place?"

"Ten miles or so." Tucker was clearly worried. "It's not the route I usually take. It's shorter in distance but the road isn't nearly as good." He was silent a moment, then repeated what Leanne had said. "Deliberately. But why? None of this makes sense to me."

No, Camp thought grimly, violence was pretty senseless to most rational people. "How well do you know Eddie?"

"Better than I want to."

Camp thought that was a cryptic answer and shot Tucker a sideways glance. "Meaning?"

"Eddie always seemed a pretty good guy in the early years when he and Marla first started coming here and later, but distracted, you know, like he didn't see anyone but his daughter. You could tell Marla was his world, and she was a crushed little girl grieving for her mama and sister. But even once he and Avery got married, he didn't have much to do with me, or Leanne when she came on board. When things started going bad, though, he wanted to hang out more at the barn, staring at the horses, and telling me how much all this was worth and how hard he'd worked for Avery to have her dream."

"Did he? Work hard, that is?"

"I'm not saying he didn't, but it wasn't at the barn or anything to do with the running of the place. The hard, physical part—that was all Avery's sweat."

"When he was talking about his hard work was he sad, angry?"

"Mostly a little drunk and kind of sloppy with it. Not falling down drunk, just … well … whining, I guess, and not realizing how weak he sounded."

Camp thought about that without answering. That was his impression of Eddie. Weak. The kind of coward who'd take a man's money and send him to pick up a horse that wasn't his to sell. Perhaps, if he'd had a little to drink for courage, even frustrated enough to put bullets through the windshield of a vehicle he already knew was empty. But did he have the nerve to run another vehicle off the road, thinking it was Avery taking her SUV back to the ranch? Yeah, maybe, but maybe not.

Would Inghram have hung around to do that? To what purpose? To scare Avery into letting him take the young horse his boss was determined to have? Again, maybe, but something wasn't adding up for him.

A strand of wire fence flashed on their left, and Tucker said, "This is the edge of the Roberts' place."

Camp took his foot off the gas. "Watch to your right," he directed tersely. And Camp watched his side of the road.

An instant later he saw headlights angled away from them. "There, on the left."

In a sharp bend ahead, the SUV was sideways some distance from the graveled edge of the road. Camp deftly swung to the shoulder but barely had the truck in park before Tucker leapt out. Camp hit the flashers and followed suit. In the distance, a siren wailed.

As he followed Tucker, Camp swiftly made note of several factors. There wasn't much of a ditch which was probably a good thing. Otherwise, the SUV would have flipped even harder during the rollover. Also good was that no trees crowded the edge of the roadway as was so often the case. The vehicle had stopped on its own and not by slamming into the unforgiving trunk of a tree.

Tucker looked up as Camp reached the car. "She's hurt and the door's jammed." There was overwhelming fear and frustration in his voice.

The window was down and Camp could see Marla's head leaned against the seat. He moved in close and spoke her name.

Marla opened her eyes and gave him a wobbly grin that faded quickly as she murmured, "Glad it was me and not Avery." Camp slipped a penlight from his pocket and her eyelids lowered as the light flashed across her face. A nasty purpling bruise already marred her temple and cheekbone. She'd need x-rays and observation at a minimum. He swept the light across the side of the SUV quickly, noting the dints and scratches from the rollover. Camp didn't ask her any of the questions crowding his mind. Time for that later. The sound of sirens was reassuringly close now.

"Marla." When she didn't respond immediately, he spoke her name more sharply.

She opened her eyes. "I'm here. Hurts."

"Where?" Camp held her gaze with his as the ambulance slid to a stop on the road beside them.

"Head … neck … shoulder. Everything." Speaking

was clearly an effort for her.

As the first EMT reached them, Camp told him, "Driver is conscious and coherent, but she took a hard hit to her head, and her door is jammed. What kind of tools do you have?"

The EMT called back to his partner and within minutes they had the door forced open and were crouched beside Marla, assessing her condition with Tucker hovering, still visibly anxious.

Camp waited patiently for the EMTs to finish their initial assessment and communicate with the local hospital. When they backed away to set up a stretcher, he moved in aware of Tucker pressed close to his side.

"Marla, I need to know. Was this an accident?" He also needed to keep her awake if he could.

Slowly, she rolled her head side to side, wincing at her own movement. "No, he made a pass, too close. I swerved, but held the road. So, he turned and came back. Nothing accidental about that."

"He?" Camp kept his tone calm and non-judgmental but he was seething inside.

"Maybe. For sure a pickup … dark colored Ford …" her voice was slurring now. Marla's eyes drifted closed. "… and the motorcycle …"

Camp had seen no sign of any other vehicle. "What motorcycle, Marla?" But Marla had slipped into unconsciousness.

Camp and Tucker watched as the skilled rescue workers carefully maneuvered Marla onto the stretcher.

"Eddie drives a black Ford." Tucker clenched his hands into fists. "I'm going with her. Then I'm going to kill that son-of-a-bitch."

Camp didn't censure the threat. He was feeling pretty violent himself. "I'll take Avery to the hospital after I make sure the sheriff can place someone to guard the ranch for a few hours." Camp intended to have someone he trusted to help with security by morning, but it would take a little while to get them mobilized.

As he watched Tucker climb into the back of the ambulance over the halfhearted protests of the EMTs, he realized this job had just taken a real personal turn for him. He knew he'd have to deal with the repercussions of that at some point. For now, his focus was Avery's safety and the safe-keeping of the animals and place she loved.

* * *

Back at the ranch, at last. What a long and unpleasant day. It may not be fair to complain, since nobody forced me into riding along with Avery. Not that there's much else a cat with my skills could do when a woman is determined to put herself in harm's way without a thought to the consequences. I can't even scold her over the habit. Humans haven't evolved enough for that.

This isn't the first time I've been frustrated that humans and cats don't share a common language. I'm clever enough to understand them, but their lower intelligence doesn't give them the same ability. Even when they speak, most of it isn't worth listening to. The horses housed in these barns can't communicate with me either and that's just as bad. I'll bet they've seen things that could crack this case, but that's no use to me if they can't fill me in.

And, of course, we have to head straight for the barn. I won't get a nibble of anything until Avery knows her horses are still safe. Though, to be honest and fair, lunch was nothing to sneeze at. Grilled fish is always a hit with me.

Leanne is pacing back and forth in front of the barn and whirls as we get close. "There you are! Why haven't you answered your phone? I've been scared sick for you!"

Judging by the shotgun in her arms and the alarm in her voice I'm thinking it's a good thing I had lunch at all. Dinner may well be late.

* * *

Avery listened in stunned silence as Leanne explained what had happened. Before she had even finished speaking, Avery turned on her heel to get back in the truck.

Leanne grabbed her wrist. "Avery, you can't. Mr. Kirkland said you were to wait here."

"*Mr. Kirkland* can go to the devil. I've got to get to Marla!" No doubt, she sounded as frantic as she felt. Her heart literally pounded against the wall of her chest. "She'll be terrified and she could be—" Her voice quit on her midsentence at the thought of losing Marla.

"Avery, listen to me. I just got off the phone with Tucker. This minute. They've taken her for x-rays of her neck and back, to be safe, but Tucker said she can move her arms, legs, fingers, and toes, and she was speaking coherently and seemed stronger. In fact, she was arguing with him and the nurses about needing to get back here to the ranch, to you. To take care of you, Avery. Tucker's got her, I promise, and," Leanne's voice turned even more grim if possible as she added, "you and I have to take care of things here."

Chapter 14

Avery's gaze scanned the pasture ahead of her. Everything was still and quiet, except for the occasional call of a night owl. She gave a quick glance over her shoulder as she began her second round of the inner perimeter fencing where groups of horses had gathered together for the night. Ridiculous as it might seem to some, the knowledge that the cat trailed steadily at her side gave her a sense that the cat had *her* back. Now and again, he trotted lightly ahead but he always circled back and around her. Someone might step out from behind a stout tree trunk up ahead, but she felt certain Callahan would know and warn her if anyone tried to sneak up behind.

Her last text from Tucker had been reassuring. Between each round of tests, Marla started another argument with the hospital staff about needing to get home. Avery's last response had been: Sit on her if you have to but she's not to leave.

She and Leanne had separated, each walking the same route in reverse, through the barns and then around the pastures. They crossed paths for a second time in front of the huddled yearlings where Avery stopped in her tracks, struck by a sudden thought she felt incredibly guilty about not having before that moment.

"Leanne, is Jason okay with you being here?"

"Jason had reserve duty this weekend. He left a few days early to spend some time with his mom and dad."

Remorse bit sharply at Avery, and she sighed. "So, he doesn't know you're risking your safety for me? Is that what you're not saying?" She knew she should send Leanne home but suspected she'd get absolutely nowhere with that argument.

Leanne's response proved her point. "This place is my livelihood and my second home, Avery, and you're way more than my employer. Jason knows I can take care of myself, like I trust him to take care of himself. I'll tell him everything when he gets home, but I don't want to distract him by telling him via cell phone because he'd want to be here—for both of us."

"And I appreciate you, I do, but God knows I don't want anything to happen to you."

"I know you don't, and I feel the same in return and—heaven knows why—but I'm glad that damned cat is marching along with you. You're the target. We both know that … you and the horses. Anything happens to me it would be collateral damage so to speak. I'm willing to take my chances to help keep you and them safe. You'd do it for me."

Avery couldn't argue because it was true. Of course, she would. All she could do was nod, eyes stinging and emotion constricting her throat. God, what a nightmare this all was.

* * *

Honestly, I wouldn't want to face up to these two determined—and frustrated—women with their loaded firearms. As a matter of fact, right about now, Avery looks very much as if she were wishing for something or someone *to shoot.*

I stop in my tracks at the sound of a vehicle approaching. The women seem to hear it a moment later or they notice me listening. Their awareness of things always seems to be a step behind mine, but then they're not cats. Should humans ever develop the talent and ability of my kind, they'd be lethal. Little chance of that happening though. I'd even bet these ladies, nice as they are, don't yet realize there are two vehicles, not one, and the second one is Camp's. If things weren't so serious, I'd have a good laugh at these female warriors easing cautiously toward the part of the drive that fronts the barns, guns at the ready.

No blue lights flashing but that's a sheriff's car at the fore. I guess that could be considered the equivalent of the cavalry arriving, but I'd put all of my money on Camp should things heat up to a battle.

* * *

Avery held her gun with barrel lowered as a deputy stepped out of each side of the patrol car.

"Evening, ladies." The driver tipped his broad-brimmed hat. "Sheriff Farley sent me and Ray to watch out for things so you could get to the hospital." He was young, clean-cut, and solemn. Whatever he may have thought about facing two women with shotguns was concealed behind a neutral expression.

His partner, older by at least a decade, eyed their weapons warily and leaned against the hood of the car, letting the younger man keep the lead.

"Have you heard anything, Matt?" Avery had known him too many years to stand on ceremony or be intimidated by his official demeanor.

"About Ms. Marla?" The younger man's lips curved the smallest bit. "Just that she's bending the ear of any and everyone standing between her and leaving that hospital. Better them than me. Rather take my chances with whatever's going down here. Ms. Marla's one determined gal when it comes to this ranch and you."

Avery drew a deep breath. It was small reassurance but she'd take what she could get. Then she tensed as another set of headlights swung toward them.

Before she could swing her gun up into position, the deputy spoke quickly. "That'd be Mr. Kirkland. He followed us out after talking with the sheriff. Said he'd take you into town once we were here."

"You'll be here all night?" She needed that reassurance. Needed to know Jack and his offspring, as well as the many talented and useful rescue horses that depended upon her, would be safe.

"Yes, ma'am. Mr. Kirkland plans to have security in place come morning but we're here until then."

Avery shot the deputy a look but held any comment for Camp who had apparently taken a great deal upon himself. She had not, would not, forget that he was investigating her. Had not, would not, forget his lack of trust in her.

Even with that, she couldn't deny the leap of her pulse as he stepped down from his truck and walked toward them with that long stride.

"Deputies." His greeting was for them, but his gaze was for Avery alone. "You'll take it from here?"

"Yes, sir. We're here until Sheriff Farley sends replacements or calls us in because you've got it covered."

Camp nodded in response, his glance like a feather touch on Avery's face. "You ready?"

"Yes," Avery said, meeting his look evenly, before turning to Leanne. "Go home and get some rest. Or, better yet, why don't you stay here since Jason's not home? At least you'd know the deputies were outside."

Leanne shook her head. "I'll be fine at home. No one's after me. Collateral damage only, remember?"

Suddenly unutterably weary, Avery told Camp, "I'm going to take a last look at Jack before we go."

Feeling his eyes on her back as she turned and scooped the cat up in her arms, Avery kept that back straight and her stride long and even, pretending with every fiber of her being that she didn't know how keenly Camp Kirkland was watching her every move.

She'd surprised the cat with her action. She felt it in the immediate stiffness of his muscles. Callahan was not your cuddly housecat. To her surprise though, he relaxed against her as she walked into the barn. But he'd matched her minute by minute through the long day which suddenly seemed never ending, and she suspected he was as tired as she. She scratched his head lightly, and again he surprised her, this time by arching his body and pushing ever so slightly against her fingers. She wondered if he were truly showing pleasure at the touch or just accepting her need for the contact. For a moment, she cradled him close as she stood in the hallway of the barn, watching as Jack put his head over the stall door to nicker a greeting.

She gently placed Callahan on the hall mat and moved closer to rub Jack's forehead, smiling because the huge horse pushed against her caress more vigorously than the cat had done. But Jack was hers, after all. He didn't allow her attentions; he demanded them as his right. It amazed her that some people failed to realize most domesticated animals craved a kind touch as much as most humans did.

For a brief moment she wrapped her arms around Jack's neck, knowing she would risk life and limb to keep him safe, always. Stepping back, she smiled tiredly down at Callahan who sat watching them both with a somewhat aloof gaze.

"Come on, mister, I'm sure Dax is wondering where you are." She turned to leave, but Callahan didn't move. Avery stopped and looked back. "Callahan, let's go."

With a deliberate look from her to Jack and back again, the cat jumped onto the canvas chair that stood outside Jack's stall. As Avery watched, Callahan settled himself into the crouched position of a cat, relaxed, but ready to move fast if speed was needed.

"You're something, aren't you," Avery said in wonderment.

Callahan blinked without moving.

"Thank you," she whispered, then left the cat to guard the animal she loved more than life.

* * *

Camp wondered if the cab of his truck felt as close, as

intimate, to Avery as it did to him. He also wondered, with a touch of bitter amusement, if she'd cooled off any since their last conversation, a conversation that now seemed eons ago instead of barely a day. From the way she sat, slightly turned so that he was presented with little more than her shoulder, he'd guessed she hadn't.

Camp had learned long ago that the best way, sometimes the only way, to get through a thing was to make a way, particularly when it wasn't going to present itself on its own.

"You may as well know I've pulled in a couple of favors. I have a security team set to arrive by daylight."

She shifted slightly so that she was facing straight ahead and shot him a glance.

Bingo. At least he had her attention, although that might not prove to be a good thing.

"I've got money. I can pay for my own security."

"Not these guys, you can't. They don't work for civilians."

The glare she gave him was incredulous. "That sounds like something more unethical than what you've accused me of doing."

He glanced from the road to her for a brief second. "First, it would only be unethical if government money was paying for their services. Second, I haven't accused you of anything. I gave you the facts of my investigation, and I'll work every bit as hard to prove you innocent as guilty."

"I am innocent, and I don't want any favors from you. I'll reimburse you, whatever this might cost." Her voice was as fierce as the expression on her face.

Camp shrugged. "Fine, if you've got a cabin in the mountains they can use for a month or two this summer, they'll be just as happy to use yours as mine."

The irritated sigh she expelled brought a curve to his lips, but he was careful not to let it become a full-fledged smile.

"Look, if we can have a truce for a little while, I'd like to talk about what happened to Marla this evening. But, first, I have a favor."

"A favor?" She sounded instantly suspicious, in spite of his request for a truce.

"I'd like to pull in that temporary guy you've got ... the soldier ... to work with the guys I'm bringing in. He can fill them in on the place, show them around, so that your team can stay focused on what they need to be doing."

"And because you think his military background would be a help." It wasn't a question.

"That, too," he admitted easily.

She hesitated. "I don't have a problem with that ... if he's willing."

Camp felt sure he would be. Soldiers were a breed apart with a feeling of responsibility for the world and those around them. He felt it. The men under his command felt it. And he had sensed it in Dax.

"I'll let you talk with him," she said, "just be sure he knows it's a request and not a command."

Camp nodded. He liked that about her. The guy might be temporary help, but she felt as keen a responsibility for him as she did for her full-time employees. "Now, about Marla's accident..."

"Leanne said some jerk ran her off the road. God, she could have been killed." Camp noticed her hands clench in her lap before she added, "And it very well could have been—and probably was—some thug associated with

Eddie's gambling debt."

"Marla said the vehicle was a dark Ford pickup. Tucker suspects it might have been her dad. Farley's going to bring him in for questioning. If he can find him."

Avery turned to face him at that. "No." Her voice was emphatic. "There's no way Eddie would do that. He adores Marla. He would never hurt his own daughter."

"She was in your SUV, remember?"

That seemed to give her momentary pause, but only for a moment. Avery shook her head in obvious bewilderment. "Things don't fit. Nothing fits. How would Eddie know Marla—or I, if he believed it was me—would be on *that* road at *that* time of day unless he followed Marla from town? That road isn't the most direct route back to the ranch. And if he *did* follow her then he'd know it was Marla and not me."

"Do you never come that way?"

"Yeah—sure I do—sometimes. There's a nice fruit and vegetable stand about midway. At least once a week or so one of us, Marla or I, will make a run to stock up. It's a pretty drive and actually not any farther, just slower because of all the curves."

Camp sorted through events of the day in his mind. Both Marla and Avery had left the ranch that morning, Avery in the ranch truck, Marla in her car. Eddie was most likely avoiding town and any face-to-face with either of them—or the sheriff. His spine didn't seem his strongest point, but then neither was his character. After Inghram's failed visit, Eddie was also likely watching the ranch as much as he could, trying to figure out his next plan, so he could easily have seen both women leave the ranch and followed them. After that, all he had to do was wait at some point, just outside of town, for Avery's return. He'd have no reason to associate Avery's SUV with Marla driving, instead of Avery. And Camp strongly suspected that the side pass at the SUV had been more spur of the moment than an actual plan.

If Camp had to guess, Eddie was running on nerves and panic, out of money, out of a plan, and doing his best to avoid the bad asses he'd let loose upon himself. He wasn't sure he completely bought in on Eddie set on murdering Avery. She seemed to be his golden goose. He had no legal claim any more but there was Marla, still, as a tie between them, and he suspected Eddie wasn't thinking all that straight about now.

He said as much to Avery. They had almost reached the turn in to the hospital when she finally spoke, and all she said was, "I don't know. I just don't know."

The little-girl-lost quality of her voice tugged as hard at Camp emotionally as her earlier kick-ass stance—caught in the headlights of his truck, legs braced, and shotgun cradled in her arm—had yanked at him physically.

He angled smoothly into a parking space near the main entrance, hearing the release of Avery's seatbelt almost before he had the truck in park. Acting on feeling far more than thought, he caught her hand in his before she could hit the door latch. The action—his hand on hers—caused her to turn in surprise, eyes wide and lips opened to question or protest or curse. He had no idea which.

Before she could do or say anything, before his mind could convince him of the greater wisdom in restraint, Camp captured those open lips with his, tugging her gently closer with his hand. To his wonderment, instead of snatching that hand away, instead of pulling back, she leaned in. He deepened the kiss, feeling things he hadn't felt in a long time, emotions mixed with purely physical lust.

His free hand cradled her face, and he fought the urge to do anything else with that hand, to explore other aspects of the woman who was an unexpected wrecking ball to his senses—at least for now.

When Avery slowly pulled away, he let her go, released her hand.

Her eyes, which had fluttered closed under his kiss, were wide again. She touched the hand he'd held to her lips, then said faintly, "Well … damn."

She fumbled to open the door behind her, eyes still locked with his, until she turned and stepped down out of the truck.

He followed her across the parking lot, fighting a grin. Yeah. Damn.

* * *

Avery watched Marla sleep, firmly pushing thoughts of Camp and the kiss they'd shared out of her mind. That kiss, and her reaction to it, was for later. Much later.

Avery had tried to make Tucker go home, back to the ranch for rest, but he'd refused. Heading with Camp to the hospital cafeteria and twenty-four-hour grill was as far as he was willing to go from Marla.

Her stepdaughter, no, not stepdaughter—*daughter*—child of her heart, even if not her body, seemed restful, but Avery's stomach was in knots once more. How could she protect her? How could her father have put her at risk?

Nurses came and went, barely making a ripple in

Avery's awareness. After a battery of tests and scans, the doctor had given an all clear the previous evening, no back or neck injury, no brain trauma. Doubtless sore muscles, aches and pains to go with the bruises, but otherwise okay. Marla had made him promise she'd be released after the night of observation he insisted upon. He'd promised on condition that Marla showed no signs of concussion through the night.

Still, Avery couldn't overcome the bone-deep fear that gripped her, not even when Marla opened her eyes and smiled. "You look a mess and I'm sure I look a hell of a lot worse." Her voice sounded a bit groggy, but her gaze was clear.

"Marla, I'm so sorry."

"Don't. Avery, just don't. None of this is your fault and we both know whose fault it is."

"I don't know how to keep you safe."

"It's your safety we have to worry about, Avery, not mine. Whoever was in that truck made a mistake this time, but we might not be so lucky the next."

"I still can't believe Eddie did this."

"I can't be sure it was my dad or his truck. Tucker's convinced, but everything happened so fast. Maybe Dad wasn't driving, maybe he was, but it's his fault either way." Marla's eyes were bleak. She closed them briefly and then opened them again. "And I'm sorry about your SUV. I guess it's back in the shop again."

"Yes, and someone is going to have to explain to me why the air bags didn't deploy."

"Actually, it's not all that uncommon. There are a lot of factors that come into play." The sound of Camp's voice from the doorway pulled Avery's gaze like a magnet. He'd been up as long as any of them, but the dark stubble where he hadn't had time to shave looked like pure, rugged male rather than the mess Marla had proclaimed *her* to be.

Avery pulled her thoughts and her attention back to Marla who had glanced up as the two men came back into the room, but closed her eyes again almost immediately. "Marla, are you hurting?"

"No, just trying to get my thoughts together. Avery, you've got to change your will so the ranch doesn't come to me if anything happens to you."

"Not going to happen." Avery was amazed at the steadiness in her voice when renewed fury at Eddie pulsed through her veins with every beat of her heart.

"You've got to. Something's broken inside my dad's head if he thinks I'd use your money to help him out of the mess he's in. That would be the one explanation for his crazy actions. Who knows what he'll do next? Or maybe he told those goons he owes that you're the one thing standing between them and repayment. And who knows what *they'll* do next?"

"Even if I was willing, and I'm not, who else would I leave it to? I'm the only child of an only child and no surviving relatives."

"Leave it to Tucker or Leanne. You're not going to be safe until he—or they—know he can't get his hands on anything through me."

"Marla, I'm not going to do that. You can tell him I did, but you helped make the ranch. It's yours as much as mine."

Marla shook her head, but Avery could tell by her stepdaughter's expression that she wasn't done with this particular argument. That was fine. Avery knew it wasn't an argument Marla would win no matter how long or loudly she pursued it.

* * *

Camp stepped out onto the curving sidewalk at the front entrance of the hospital while Avery helped Marla dress for the trip home. The doctor would have preferred to keep her one more night, but Marla was adamant about her release, reminding him of his promise, and he finally conceded.

The morning air was still faintly cool, but that wasn't going to last long. Late summer had hit central Alabama with a vengeance.

Preoccupied as Camp was, his subconscious registered the shiny Goldwing barely a split second before his conscious. The man stowing his helmet ignored Camp until he spoke.

"You were at the courthouse." Camp had no doubt. The bulge of muscle across shoulders, neck and back. The dark, buzz-cut hair. Camp's brain recorded the tiny tattoo on the back of one hand. It was an odd design, apropos of nothing that Camp could tell. He'd want to look that up later, though he suspected it had little or nothing to do with the matter at hand.

The other man turned, a placid expression belying the sharp gaze. "Was I?"

"And at the scene of a wreck last night."

The expression tightened. "You are mistaken."

No street thug, this one. His speech was smooth with no hint of accent. His clothes mirrored his bike. Expensive.

"I'll be watching to see if you turn up anywhere near

New Hope Ranch. It would be a mistake on your part."

"Threatening me is a mistake on yours. A much worse mistake."

Camp watched as the other man retrieved the helmet he'd just stowed and threw a leg over his bike.

Camp smiled grimly. "As long as I don't see you again there won't be any problem."

He stood back as the motorcycle engine caught and roared. Just as he'd made note of the tattoo, he quickly memorized the tag. He'd share the tag and his concerns with Farley.

The rider didn't look back as he wheeled his bike smoothly into the flow of traffic on the street in front of the hospital.

Chapter 15

I'll admit I'm impressed. Not that I thought Marla would be the type of girl to walk around all pale and weak after her night at the hospital. I'd even bet she never skipped school to miss a test as a kid, either. She beat Avery out the door this morning, stooping to give me a stroke on her way past with that morning cup of brew—coffee or joe or java or by whatever name it's called—most humans seem to enjoy. The drink is a puzzle, and I have to think the taste is more appealing than the odor, which while not unpleasant, is still nothing to brag about.

Marla herself is somewhat of a puzzle as well; at least I find certain aspects of her behavior puzzling. That light stroke along my back, for one, which she never fails to extend. It's not for show, I'm sure of that because there's usually not anyone about to witness, such as now. I never would've taken her for a cat human. Not that she's ever disagreeable toward me. She never is. It's more that she doesn't seem to notice me much of the time. In fairness, maybe that's my pride talking. I know that not all humans recognize the depths of a cat's intellect and talents. But vanity aside, the Egyptians knew what they were doing when they proclaimed the cat as the great god.

Avery at least has come to understand and appreciate my abilities and there she is now, moving with that quiet energy of hers. And nice person that she is, her first move is to open the door for me to stroll in. It's that awareness and consideration of my needs that seems lacking in Marla, as it is in so many other humans. I'm patient as she scrambles my eggs. And she doesn't pull down some old chipped bowl for me. I'm always served from the same dinnerware as she serves herself. It's the little things that matter.

Oh, rats! I hear the sound of another truck and trailer entering the premises. I hope it isn't a return of Inghram. I've had enough of his unpleasantness. A quick glance at Avery reassures me on that score. Though she heard as well, her expression remains serene. At ease, I set my attention to the plain but filling dish in front of me. Whatever the humans are about this morning, I have at least these few moments of peace before I once more turn my attention to pulling the latest pieces of the puzzle together. Marla's wreck was no accident caused by a careless driver. Whoever forced the SUV into a rollover is part of the threats that face New Hope Ranch.

Is the ex-husband childishly acting out his anger at having lost the court battle? Was the intent to scare and intimidate or was it a serious attempt at murder? Or was it Inghram, or a hired hand, at the wheel? Should I anticipate a next move as being some threat in the guise of a warning or blackmail attempt from one or the other of them? When all is said and done, more often than not, it really is money at the root of all evil.

And, I didn't enjoy my eggs half as much as I would have if I hadn't been mulling over the possibilities. But now that I've finished,

I'll take a pass through the barns. I don't doubt that the security team Camp engaged is as vigilant as any human could be, but—after all— they're only human.

* * *

Avery waited as the woman clad in jeans and tee shirt stepped out of the big rig. "Renee, it's so good to see you again."

Renee returned the smile. "I'm glad you called me. The video you sent of the mare was pretty impressive. She has a nice stride and a quick turn and I know I can trust your judgement on her disposition." She turned a sweeping gaze on the barns and paddocks. "I love this place. It's so well laid out. My barns are such a hodge-podge, us throwing things together as we needed them."

Avery laughed. "It was sometimes hard not to do that myself but I stuck to my vision, even though it sometimes meant waiting until the money was right to move ahead on the next phase. And how is the rodeo business?"

"Wickedly paced. I made the finals again, hauled twelve outside horses and three of my own. I thought I'd be slowing down by now, but ... busy is better."

Avery had met Renee a few years earlier. She knew how difficult life had been for her.

"I did appreciate the note you sent." Renee's voice was quiet, and Avery caught a glimpse of the shadows that lingered in her eyes. "Now, about this mare."

"She's in Barn One." They fell into step together as Avery continued to talk about the horse. "Tucker has given her a clean bill of health, x-rays and all. No sign of bone chips or spurs that would give you any problems later on. I have no idea where she came from or what sent her to the kill pen. She was a rack of bones with sad, sad eyes but no one who saw her then would recognize her now. This girl is gorgeous."

"Personality?"

"Sweet but not what I'd call peaceful. She's playful, too much so for most of our clients, though a few of the more skilled riders enjoy her as much as I do. More than once, when I'd watch her racing across the pasture, dodging the other horses in some game of her own, I'd think of you. It was Leanne who finally accepted that she needed a different kind of job. All of us agree we could find ways and places for her to be useful here but we're not where she'll be happiest."

They stepped into the cool of the barn, and Avery led the way to a wide stall. "We call her Bella."

At the sound of her voice, Bella immediately abandoned the rubber ball hung from a tether for her entertainment and stepped closer, thrusting her head over the stall door and nickering a greeting.

Renee moved close, rubbing her hand over the broad forehead, clearly delighted when the mare pushed back against the caress in pleasure. "What eyes, what beautiful eyes. Where's her halter?"

Avery chuckled, taking the halter and lead from a horseshoe hook outside the stall. She handed it over and stepped aside, giving control to the accomplished horsewoman she knew Renee to be.

Renee led the mare to her trailer and spent a moment brushing and grooming. "I know she doesn't need it, she absolutely gleams, but I need a moment for her to get to know me and to figure out which saddle will be most comfortable to her."

Avery would have done the same. Saddles were always careful choices of feel and fit for both horse and rider.

After lifting and checking each hoof, Renee saddled the mare with what Avery could see was well-used but meticulously-cared for tack. Minutes later, horse and rider were in the paddock. Renee spent time slowly warming up the mare's muscles before moving her seamlessly from one gait to another. Skillfully, perfectly in sync, they executed a series of side-passes, small circles, spins, and backing. After half an hour, Renee was grinning, her delight evident.

In the time Renee had been working the mare, Tucker had moved to stand beside Avery, then Leanne and finally Marla. They watched together as Renee walked the mare to cool her out.

"From that expression, I'd say Bella may have found her forever home." Leanne sounded delighted.

"Well, at least she'll be off the feed and vet bill," Marla commented.

"She's earned her keep in the time she's been here," Leanne returned quickly.

Though aware of the exchange, Avery didn't comment on it. Leanne's tone had been a little defensive, perhaps, though Marla hadn't been caustic in the least. It had been a simple statement of fact. Marla was the most practical of them, and Avery knew someone had to be. She and Leanne were less so but they were still cautious not to overextend the ranch. It was the livelihood, after all, for all of them. It allowed them the opportunity to do what they loved and make a better-than-average living doing it while helping both the humans and the horses that crossed their path. It was a hurtful fact that they couldn't save everyone and everything. It just wasn't possible.

Renee was still smiling as she led the mare toward them. She nodded when Avery asked if she remembered her team. "I do, and it's good to see you all again. What a handle this gal has! Who gets the glory for that?"

Leanne, who'd ridden her most, stepped forward. "She came to us that way. All we had to do was put some weight back on her and rebuild her muscle."

"Well, I'm completely won over. How long has she been here?"

"A little over six months," Marla chimed.

Renee stared straight at Avery. "I want her, no doubt. I know you don't sell your horses. I remember that from my first trip here and my first rescue, who has won me a ton of money by the way. Still and all, I'd like to reimburse you for what you have in her."

The figure she named had Avery shaking her head. "That's way more than what we put into her health wise, plus I truly can't sell any of them. I called you because I thought she'd be a better fit for your world than ours. She's free to you because I know you'll bring her back to us if she doesn't work out."

"Then let me give you a donation for another rescue or two."

Avery sighed and cut the amount by more than half, adding. "Truly, though, we don't need anything." But the money could help rescue another horse or two. Everything helped.

"It's more than fair to me. If she doesn't take to barrels, I'll bring her home again. But I'm betting my heart she'll love running drums. Her build is pure athlete and her mind seems sound. Eager but not agitated."

"She doesn't have registration papers," Marla cautioned, "at least not that came with her. All we have is a piece of paper giving ownership to us with her name and description. I suspect she has good bloodlines. We couldn't find any way of tracing them. We don't try with the geldings but we do with the mares in case we want to breed them. It helps to know what genetics to avoid and what to blend together."

"I understand that. There are some bloodlines out there I don't want anywhere in my string, but, truthfully, I don't need papers. I make my living competing, for myself and for others, not buying and selling or breeding. A simple bill of sale is all I need."

"I'll get that ready while you unsaddle," Marla offered.

Avery gave Marla a smile of thanks, more for not commenting on the unexpected offer of money than the preparation of the necessary paperwork. Leanne wouldn't take kindly to a witty zing about recouping expenses for a rescue horse that hadn't been as useful to their program as the others. Avery hadn't a doubt that all of her team were close and had each other's back, but they weren't above sniping at each other over differences of opinion.

Avery's gaze tracked Marla as she walked away. The girl had covered her bruises with makeup, which she rarely wore, and Avery suspected that was more to keep concern and comments at bay than from vanity. Otherwise, Avery could see no sign of the soreness she knew the girl had to be feeling in her back and shoulders and neck. The doctor had warned that the third day would be the worst so Avery would be extra watchful in the morning. For now, though, Marla seemed to be moving well and Avery let go of a little more of her anxiety.

She was on the point of turning back to Renee when she saw Marla change her angle to intercept Camp who was walking their way. The sight of him made her heart leap a bit. She'd done her best to put the memory of that kiss from her mind but it had crept in at odd moments and came flooding back now. *I'll work as hard to prove you innocent as guilty*, he'd said. But would he? Could she trust him? Trust these feelings she didn't want to have for him? Eddie had been a bitter, bitter lesson, but Camp was a different kind of man. One that appealed to her on every level, she had to admit.

When Camp shifted his gaze to hers, she realized she was staring at him. She realized something else as well, Marla was still facing him and there was something in the line of her body, in the way she leaned slightly forward, and in the tilt of her chin that shot a line of discomfort straight through her as if she'd been caught eavesdropping on a personal moment. She shifted her attention quickly away, not returning the quick smile Camp had sent her.

When she glanced back a moment later, Camp was staring after Marla, and she wondered what would be revealed if she could see his eyes. One thing was sure, she would never be in competition with any woman for a man's attention, particularly not with one she considered as much her daughter as any person could ever be.

* * *

Camp watched Marla walk away, still unsure what that exchange with her had been about. She'd commented to him that she'd met his security team—Rick and Jeremiah— but her tone had conveyed that she was unimpressed by their quiet, polite manners. She'd been civil when she asked Camp if he considered them a match for the trouble hounding the ranch, but her expression made it clear that she, personally, did not. Camp had assured her they were professionals and known for success, not failure. He had no intention of telling her they were retired Special Forces. He didn't believe anything he said would sway Marla's opinion, anyway.

She made no secret of the fact that she was suspicious of Camp, his motives, his reasons for being there, and—most pointedly—his interest in Avery. She was protective, fiercely protective of Avery. Camp didn't find that unusual from all he knew about the relationship between them, but he did find the vehemence of it a little off-putting. He had a sense that there was more than concern in Marla's attitude toward Avery, perhaps a hint of jealousy and a determination to keep Avery's affection to herself. He would expect that in a child or even a teen, all things considered, but he didn't expect it in what appeared to be a strong and self-sufficient young adult. But he knew as well as anyone that there was a reason for the old adage that appearances could be deceiving.

Putting thoughts of Marla aside, Camp walked toward Avery, keeping his stride quiet and easy, though his thoughts were anything but. He wanted her. He wasn't supposed to, and wasn't sure what to do about it, but it was there. He supposed the first necessity—beyond keeping her and everything she loved safe—was proving her innocence in whatever financial shenanigans her ex had going on for the past year. The second necessity, and it was a necessity to him at least, was to convince her that he was someone she could trust, someone she could count on. That, he suspected, was going to be a hard sell when her last example had been the likes of Eddie Danson.

He found no lingering remembrance of their kiss in the steady glance she turned his way as he reached the paddock. In fact, she seemed even more remote now than before that moment of undeniable heat in his truck.

Camp smiled, nodded, shook hands through the introduction with Renee Sumrall. Then he hung back, quiet and patient, watching as a pretty mare was loaded onto a long, aluminum trailer. Papers were exchanged as Marla rejoined the group.

A short while later, Renee Sumrall pulled out of the drive. Marla shot Camp a look over Avery's shoulder. It wasn't hostile, but it wasn't friendly either. For a moment, he wondered if she would deliberately pull Avery away on some pretext, but after a moment's hesitation, she turned and walked away with Tucker and Leanne.

Camp's patience was rewarded when Avery turned, saw him still standing there, and walked his way.

She stopped in front of him and said, "Hi."

To Camp's amusement she seemed as if she didn't quite know what to say now that she had given into the impulse to seek his company, and he was pretty sure it had been impulse. The sunlight caught in her hair, pulling hints of bronze from the coffee-colored curls. He fought the urge to touch an errant tendril.

"Good morning," he said in turn. "I'm headed into town shortly. Need anything?"

"Not that I can think of."

"Mind if I pick up some steaks for that big-ass grill you never use? I'd like to pull my team together with yours for shift turnover every evening until we get things sorted out.

Might as well get everyone fed while we're at it."

This time the hint of a smile on her lips reached her eyes, not big and bright like he hoped one day to see, but at least it was there. "Sure. I have a few clients until early afternoon, but there are peas from my garden in the freezer that I can put on slow simmer."

"Sounds good to me." And because he couldn't help himself, he reached out to touch her face, just once, very lightly.

* * *

Camp used the drive into town to sort through his thoughts. What he suspected, what he thought he knew, what he knew for certain, as well as some facts and figures from files he'd studied and then restudied.

Someone had signed Avery's name to government issued payments for veterans. Eddie was the most likely culprit because he damned sure didn't believe Avery had done that. And it was Eddie who'd siphoned money on a regular basis through an ATM card, Eddie who was in financial straits. Avery, along with the ranch, was solvent but she'd, no doubt, been unable to grow her business as quickly as she could have done.

He knew Marla had money from her mother's insurance as well as from her share of the ranch proceeds. Her car payment and cell phone were automatically deducted from her checking account. Occasionally, she bought clothes, mostly jeans and shirts and boots, but not often and not extravagantly. She was as solvent as Avery and wanted Avery to remove her from her will.

Tucker made a better-than-average living at the ranch

and, like Marla, he saved most of his earnings and lived well within his means. Leanne and her husband were renting a small ranch house while saving money for a home of their own. Still young and childless, they indulged once a week or so in dinner with drinks, beer for him, a glass of wine for her. Their vehicles were well-used and equally well-maintained. No large debt, no large luxuries.

Eddie was the financial gap. He gambled wildly and, while he didn't lose big, he lost regularly. Interspersed with the frequent losses were the occasional large wins, just often enough to keep him coming back for one more try.

In addition to siphoning money from the ranch until Avery caught him at it, Eddie had cheated the owner of a lumber store and taken money for a horse he didn't own. Both actions made him a prime candidate for prosecution. With no reliable means of income, he'd be getting desperate now.

Marla may not have positively identified her father as the driver who'd run her off the road, but her suspicion was more than clear. She believed him at least capable of killing Avery to get his hands on the ranch, the horses, and the money through her. So far, neither the sheriff nor his deputies had been able to find Eddie for questioning. Was Marla beginning to wonder if her own life would be in danger if her father became desperate enough and she withheld money from him?

Camp parked at the edge of town and walked through it as he had a couple of days earlier, but this time with a different end in mind. Before, he'd been hunting for clues to a way to clear Avery's name with the government and ensure she was safe from her ex-husband's enemies before heading back to D.C.

This time, he was contemplating the town through an altered viewpoint, wondering if this was a place he could live with a woman who had built a life and a business here, a business that enabled her to live well and help others— both horse and human. He'd never ask her to leave. He wasn't ready to talk marriage and she wasn't ready to hear it, but if he didn't think this was a place he could make his home, it was a conversation that would never happen. He wouldn't do that to himself or to her.

It was a peaceful place, a pretty place, with parks and restaurants and theaters, with businesses and shops and boutiques, not too far from larger towns with brighter nightlife but not too close to them either. So where, exactly, did that realization leave him?

He'd never been tempted to marry, and he wasn't sure why that was. Over the years, he'd had a series of love interests, some more serious than others, but he'd let each slip away and hadn't looked back with more than a twinge of regret. That twinge was not because he'd wanted forever-after with any of them but because he'd truly cared about each one—just not enough to propose they tie their lives together forever. And eventually, each one of them had accepted that—some with tears and melodrama, some with a hug and a smile of regret—and moved on to a man more inclined to think in terms of forever.

It was true there were times he wondered what his life would have been like with a son to play ball with, a daughter to take to some father-daughter middle school dance. In the thick of action, though, as he held men dying with whispered regrets and sorrow over a family left to grieve, he knew he'd made the right decision for himself. But that was then.

Now? Now was different. Now there was Avery.

He passed the sheriff's office, but didn't drop in. He and the sheriff had already talked by phone about the biker, the tag number on his Goldwing, and his odd tattoo. If Ben Farley had learned anything new, he'd know it. He had that much faith in the lawman and suspected the lawman now had that much faith in him. They were on the same side in this quest to return Avery to a place without turmoil and without dread that something or someone she loved would be hurt or taken.

Just as he'd decided to return to his truck and head to the local meat market, a young woman stepped out of the feed and tack store, clearly intent on locking up. Camp was surprised when she called out to him. "Aren't you the guy out at New Hope Ranch? The government guy looking at the place for some kind of veterans' program?"

"I am." He introduced himself and shook the hand she offered so casually.

"I'm Kim. Are you headed back to the ranch now?"

"Yeah, I am, after another stop."

"Great. I have some calendars I'd love for you to take to Avery if you don't mind. She doesn't come into town that often—none of them do—and I'm dying for her to see what the photographer did. They're right on the counter. It won't take me a minute to step back in to get them."

She was already unlocking the door, and Camp doubted she even realized she hadn't given him a chance to agree or refuse.

When she stepped back out, she was beaming. She handed him the top one on the stack. "Isn't that place gorgeous?"

He supposed it was, but all he saw was the woman

astride a magnificent horse he recognized as Jack, and he knew he'd found his answer. She was half turned from the camera so that the photographer had caught little more than the lift of her chin and curve of her cheek with that tumble of hair to her shoulders. Her back was slim, straight and he could see the strength in her as much as the beauty. Yeah, for her, he'd live here in this pleasant little town—or anywhere else she chose to be.

Chapter 16

True to her word, Avery had tender peas simmering in vegetable stock. It had been a busy afternoon. She'd worked with three clients, pulled salad greens and vegetables from her garden, showered, dithered over makeup, no makeup, and back again. She suspected the kitchen smelled more like the bacon she'd fried to season the peas than the light fragrance of her soap.

When Camp opened the back door without knocking, it felt right and she tried not to let that bother her. Just go with it, she told herself as she glanced over her shoulder at him from her place by the stove.

He placed the steaks on the quartz counter, followed by a bag of what most assuredly were hand-selected baking potatoes. Her eyes widened at the amount of both. "How many armies are you feeding?"

"One small one," he answered with a grin. He stepped closer to peer into the cast iron roaster she was stirring. "Oh, man, I don't know when I last had fresh corn creamed by hand and not dumped out of a can. I almost swung by the open-air market for salad things, but it looks like we don't need them."

She liked his grin, realized she liked it too much, so turned her attention back to the roaster of corn. "Need or not, we'll have those salad things, but fresh from my backyard instead, already washed, and in the fridge. There's beer in there, too, if you're interested."

"I am." He pulled one out, saw the Chardonnay chilling, and asked, "Wine?"

She hesitated … not a date, not a date, not a date … then said, "Sure."

Beer and wine and steaks wouldn't make it a date. It was a military strategy session, nothing more. Even so, she sensed the change in him. She wasn't sure what that change was, what it portended, if anything. They'd shared meals early on—before she realized she was in his line of fire for assigning guilt—but that was then and this was now, and now felt very different.

She pretended not to notice as he rummaged through her cabinets, passing up her everyday wine goblets to find what he wanted in a lighter-than-air crystal tinted a rich emerald green.

He pulled the cork on the wine with quiet expertise and poured. When he handed her the glass, he smiled. "Almost the same shade as the green in your eyes."

And her heart tilted. She took the glass he held out to her, their fingers barely brushing, but the touch, soft as butterfly wings, had her heart dropping as if on the wildest roller coaster.

* * *

Once Camp started the grill, the team started gathering. With her part done, Avery took her wine glass to the double-glider, dropped her sandals to the deck, and tucked her feet under her. Callahan bounded agilely to the seat beside her and curled up, waiting in anticipation of steak, she supposed.

Tucker came first, sniffing appreciatively at the scent of hickory flavored charcoal. "Oh, man, I know that stuff ain't good for you, but it's so worth it."

Camp smiled, and suggested he grab a beer from the kitchen. Avery lifted a brow and smiled as Tucker stepped in and grabbed a bottle and a glass and returned just as quickly. He took a seat on the back step and poured his beer into the glass.

"I don't think grilling over gas is considered any healthier than charcoal," Camp offered.

Tucker frowned at that, considering, and then gave a quick nod. Apparently, all he cared about in that regard was the steak. "You learn anything new or interesting while you were in town?"

"Not new, but interesting. Just reaffirmed some things in my mind."

Avery wondered what that meant but had no intention of asking him. She thought Tucker might ask, but Marla walked up and, as usual, there went Tucker's attention. She'd smile if she thought Marla had any real interest in him. As it was, she feared Tucker was in for a real heartbreak if he got any more serious. She hoped he wouldn't. The team worked well together. A failed romance or broken heart could ruin that. And she wasn't entirely selfish in her hope. Tucker didn't deserve heartbreak. He deserved the love of his life to love him back. And there she went again, believing in fairy tales.

Leanne arrived next, her husband with her. "Avery, hey, Leanne said I was welcome to join y'all."

Avery stood and gave him a hug. "You're always welcome here, Jason, and you have as much right as any of us to know what's going on. Especially now. This can't be what you expected to come home to." She still felt guilty that Leanne was at any kind of risk because of her problems.

Jason had wide shoulders, a full head of dark hair without a hint of curl to it and dimples that Leanne had laughingly told her he preferred to call creases. Leanne went straight to the kitchen to get them a drink, and Jason pulled two of the wooden chairs closer to the action.

For a moment, it seemed to Avery that the atmosphere was turning almost festive, at least until Marla stepped out of the house with a glass of ice water in her hand. The glance she gave Camp as he stood at the grill was as chill as the drink she carried as she moved close to Avery.

"Are you still feeling sore?" Avery asked, scooting over to make room. Callahan leapt to the deck, not looking back at the two of them, as he curled his tail around him.

"Hardly at all. Quit worrying." It was an order but Marla said the words lightly with a smile. She glanced around. "Are we eating out here? It's not too hot for a change."

"I'd cleared the dining table of paperwork for us, but we could, I suppose."

Before the suggestion could become a debate, Camp's security duo arrived.

With the potatoes roasting on the grill and the group settled in various places, Camp took the lead, giving quick introductions to those who hadn't yet met. Avery immediately liked the two men Camp had brought in but she was uncertain they could be effective when no one could guess where the next risk lay. She wasn't surprised when Marla said as much.

"We don't know who or what my dad has turned loose on us or even what he might decide to do next. Jesus, running Avery's car off the road? There's no talking to him. I can't get through to him at all."

"When was the last time you talked with him?" Camp asked.

Marla thought a minute. "Two days ago, I think. I tried twice today. He's not answering his phone. Guess he doesn't want to hear it was his own daughter he nearly killed."

Marla's voice held deep bitterness, and Avery's heart ached for her. Clearly, Marla had come to accept Tucker's opinion that it had been Eddie who had run her off the road. Avery reached for her hand but all Marla allowed was one quick squeeze. Marla wasn't—had never been—what Avery thought of as a hugger. Even so, the fierce pressure of Marla's hand in hers, however brief, held a wealth of emotion. Feelings Avery knew Marla rarely put into words.

"Even if the truck was your father's," Camp said evenly, "he may not have been the driver."

Marla stared at him, perplexed. "What are you suggesting? That someone could have stolen his truck and then tried to run me—or Avery—off the road? That doesn't make sense."

"Depends on who was driving." Jeremiah had a quiet, low voice, but one that commanded immediate attention. Avery suspected he'd never have to shout to be heard. "Your father has made some serious enemies. He owes them money, and they want what's due them."

Avery realized what Jeremiah was hinting at before Marla did and watched as understanding dawned.

"You think someone did something to him? Hurt him and stole the truck?"

Marla stood and began pacing, nearly stumbling over Callahan in her distraction.

Glancing at Camp, Avery's heart dropped as she realized the men suspected just that. Marla was angry at her father now, but Avery had no doubt she would be devastated to lose him. Since the deaths of her sister and mother, he was her last living blood relative. From his expression, Camp, at least, thought it might well come to that.

* * *

Rather than risk being trampled by clumsy feet, I think I'd be smart to take a turn around the barns and paddock. Add to that, with the humans all gathered in one place, the villain would have free rein should he decide on an attack in the next bit. Not that I think he will, mind you, nor does Camp, I'm confident. If he had concerns, he would've taken additional precautions. Still, a bit of recon wouldn't be a bad idea, especially while the prime steak I'm anticipating is 'resting' on the kitchen counter. I took a peek earlier and, though I'm confused why a dead cow requires rest, the humans in my life all appear to think that a necessity prior to displaying their grilling expertise.

I pause long enough for Dax to run his hand down my back as he arrives to join what I hope is a crackerjack team that Camp has brought in. We shall see. If they're less than they should be, I have faith that Dax will help turn things to right. He's that kind of a guy.

It's a perfect night, less humid than it has been. I can almost catch a scent of autumn on the evening breeze, but I know for sure there are several more weeks of brutal heat to come. I don't sense any agitation among the small herds of the young, or the old, in their respective pastures. All seems quiet there as well as within the barns. It may be a waste of time and a bore to make another reconnaissance, but the steaks aren't yet on the grill so nothing lost if I do.

There are times that boredom can be appealing, and a stroll is good exercise. I have to keep my edge. Fighting crime and solving problems can be draining if a person—or cat—isn't in tip-top shape.

After strolling along the pastures, I find myself at what Avery refers to as Barn Three. It's late enough that all of the child-prodigy equines have been fed and, once fed, are snoozing on a full belly. Barn Two is much the same. Large heads hang over stall doors, gazing at me curiously as I pass by. A few of the animals doze in a corner and couldn't care less that I'm here for their protection.

All appears as it should be, yet I have this sense of disquiet, that all is not as it should be. And, in Barn One, I find exactly the sort of thing I dread to see. A note fastened to a stall front. Not any stall but that of Avery's favored equine, Jack.

I find nothing concerning about any of the various scents that cling to the small area around the stall. It's clear to me, though, that this needs the humans' immediate attention. These people leave each other reminders or information upon a whiteboard with colored markers at the front of each barn. They don't use pen and paper and thumb tacks on stall fronts.

* * *

Avery looked almost relieved when Camp decided the grill was ready and refused to talk business for the next little while. He declared the steaks he'd hand-picked were prime beef and not to be relegated to back-seat. Sensing her stress at the turn the conversation had taken, he deftly changed the subject altogether, effectively distracted the entire group by producing the ranch calendars he'd picked up while in town.

He glanced willingly at the pictures on each page, though the ones that caught and held his attention were the six that featured Avery with six different animals. Even he could tell that her attire had been matched to suit both tack and horse. Sleek sophistication paired with a tall, athletic hunter-jumper. Bling, as Leanne laughingly tagged it, when she sat astride a compact quarter horse under western saddle. Jaunty Irish togs as she leaned lovingly against the little Connemara she'd given away to a young boy in need.

Even he had to acknowledge the stark elegance of the photograph of Marla that Tucker called to his attention. Her hair was tucked completely under a hat and the photographer had been positioned so that the camera caught her profile against a darkening sky of sunset plum and lavender. The horse, heavily muscled, had been captured dramatically between one movement and the next.

But looking from the photograph of Marla to the inner-lit beauty that was Avery, he thought *no contest*. He could see her relaxing into the quiet camaraderie of the group but the respite proved brief. Callahan leapt onto the porch with a yowl, drawing everyone's attention to him. He circled Avery's feet until she stood and placed her glass of wine on a small table.

"What is it, Callahan? What's wrong?"

"Seriously, Avery?" Marla said with a half-laugh. "He's hungry as usual and smelled the steaks on the grill."

"I don't think so." Avery stood for a moment, staring into Callahan's gold eyes, then stepped down from the porch. "I'll be back when I've checked out what's stressed him."

She seemed barely aware of Camp's handing over the tongs to Tucker. "They're ready. Get everyone served, and we'll be back."

He followed close by her side as Callahan led the way. Her pace quickened and Camp realized with a silent dread where the cat was leading them. "Jack!" He heard the urgency in her voice but all was quiet in the barn and there was her beloved horse, safe, his head thrust over the stall door as usual at her approach.

Camp slowed as he saw the folded paper tacked to Jack's door, right below the handle where the horse could not reach and worry it free. He hesitated, then pulled it loose, handing it to Avery, who had been solely focused on the animal.

Slowly, she read it aloud. "You will connect with any buyer who contacted you in the past asking to purchase the offspring of Flying Jackanapes and you will now offer them—all of them—for sale. You will receive drop off instructions for the money from each sale. If you fail to sell them or fail to produce the money, the animals will die, one by one. You have 24 hours to make the first offer, no more, no less."

She looked at Camp in absolute terror and surprised him, as much as he suspected she surprised herself, by moving into the shelter of his waiting arms. Camp couldn't help himself as he brushed his lips against her temple. Her action proved that she trusted him, even if only instinctively, trusted that he would help keep her horses safe. And he would, if it took his last ounce of effort—that much he knew.

"I don't know how to make this stop, how to make it all go away," she admitted, whispering the words against his chest.

"Yeah, well I do," he said, and prayed that she would believe him, trust him.

* * *

Marla stood up as they walked back toward the gathering.

"You found something after all, didn't you?" Her gaze searched Avery's face. "The horses? They're all right?"

Avery handed her the threatening note, and Marla blanched upon reading it. Without missing a beat, Marla shot Camp a hard glare. "So much for your crackerjack security team," she said derisively, but her voice softened as she turned back to Avery. "What are we going to do?"

"I've got the beginnings of a plan worked out," Camp said. "We've got at least a day before there will be another move."

For a moment, Avery thought—feared—Marla would explode, the anger was so clear on her face. And Avery understood, truly she did. If anything, it would appear to Marla that Camp was interfering far more than he was helping, but unexpectedly, Marla nodded. "That's probably true. The note says twenty-four hours."

She turned to Avery, studied her quietly for a moment.

"You're completely wiped, aren't you?" she finally asked softly. "We both are, I guess. We need a mental break. Let's get away, at least for a bit, maybe trail ride tomorrow, talk through our options and come up with a plan. Do you trust Mr. Kirkland to keep an eye on things for a few hours in the morning?"

Avery heard the disregard for any plan Camp had in the making as well as the challenge. She knew Camp would have heard it as well, but he responded calmly. "I can handle things here, Marla."

Avery wasn't sure that Marla was convinced, but somehow, Avery was. What she wasn't sure about was being away from the ranch, especially now when events seemed to be escalating, and she said as much.

"We don't have to be gone too long." Marla's tone was almost pleading. "Leave early and back by lunch, maybe? You need that time out … and so do I."

The girl rarely asked for anything. It was that, more than anything, that convinced Avery, and she nodded. "Just a few hours, though."

She was glad she'd yielded when Marla smiled and took a deep breath. "Good. That's good. We'll both be better for it."

Chapter 17

I'm uneasy about the notion of Marla and Avery out in the open spaces of the ranch with no protection and so, I suspect, is Camp. On the other hand, I can understand Avery needing a 'mental break' as Marla put it. As weighty as my sense of accountability toward my charges, I can only imagine the strain of having sole responsibility for the livelihood of three full-time employees—with Marla being family as much and more than employee—along with the safety of all of these large animals enjoying, as am I, the pre-dawn coolness.

Everything seems peaceful, at least for now. Camp's security duo has been as vigilant as he could want through the night, but my anxiety still grows, which could be due to nothing more than lack of sleep. I've pushed over my own limits there. One last swing through the barn and past Jack's stall and then a much-needed power nap. I can't allow myself any more of a rest than that, not until I sort through my uneasiness.

I'm happy to find that all is as serene inside as it is outside and Avery's favorite chair is looking cozy there at Jack's stall door. All I need is a few moments rest and I'll be ready to go again.

Before I settle, I see a light on in what these horse humans call a tack room, where saddles and bridles and various other equipment and supplies are kept. With the memory of the devastation on the evening of my arrival here still strong in my mind, I move to the doorway on silent paws.

Odd. It's Marla, who really should be sleeping at this hour, particularly so soon after her nasty wreck. Yet, here she is running her hands over the attachments that make up a saddle, the various straps and buckles and screws. Her expression is intense but not tense. As I watch, she turns from one saddle to another and repeats the scrutiny.

I hear a sound and press against the wall as I turn to look down the long barn hallway. Ah, it is one of our borrowed law-enforcement, striding quickly but surprisingly lightly toward the glow of the light. He hesitates as he recognizes one of the occupants of the ranch.

"It's late. Is something wrong?"

Marla's laugh is a brittle sound. "Other than the fact that I haven't slept since this mess with my father started? No, everything's lovely. Avery and I are going riding this morning out in the hills on two of the younger horses. Broke but still fairly green. It's good for them and something we routinely do."

"But?"

"But just recently Avery took a bad tumble because tack had been deliberately damaged. I've found a piece or two since then that I've had repaired. We always use western saddles out in the hills and at four a.m. my eyes opened as I realized I hadn't checked these since … well since then."

"Everything seem okay?"

"Yes, everything's fine."

He nods, hearing clearly as I do, the dismissal in her tone. He can't know that she has shared more with him than is typical. In my time here, I've discovered Marla to be a young lady of surprisingly few words.

As he exits, I glance back at Marla as she slides first one, then another gleaming rifle into two scabbards and attaches each carefully to the saddles in front of her. Clearly, she expects danger or is at the least direly worried about the possibility—so much so that she wants Avery as well as herself to have a weapon. It is only a bit reassuring that her movements are sure and confident. This is not her first outing with firearms, I think, as I recall the shotgun she carried on their previous ride.

Marla seems not to notice me as she strides from the tack room and the barn. I glance at the cozy chair in front of Jack's stall but I've an inexplicable, yet solid, feeling of foreboding that may not allow me to nap.

* * *

Avery opened her eyes to an immediate sweep of tension. As much as she and Marla needed a time out, Avery knew she'd just carry her worries with her. She consoled herself they weren't leaving the property and would only be gone a few hours, at most. No more time than a drive into town for supplies. If something happened here, they could turn back.

She trusted, absolutely, that Camp would keep things safe here in her absence. That trust amazed her but also gave her an immense sense of relief. And Marla was right, they couldn't put their world on hold or fall apart in dealing with this new threat. Nor could she be sure this would be the last threat to come at her.

It was time to move forward. With Eddie no longer siphoning off income, she believed she could soon see her way clear to either increase their barn crew or turn the three, part-time barn help into permanent positions. There were pluses and minuses to either option, and she made a mental note to discuss the opportunities with Marla during their morning ride.

Avery showered quickly and wasn't the least surprised to hear clatter from the kitchen. She walked into the room to find Marla, dressed as she was in jeans and tee-shirt, at the stove top, flipping a toasted cheese sandwich. Marla turned to give her a half-smile. "I knew you'd be up early."

"And yet you're up even earlier. Did you sleep well?"

"Fairly well. You?"

Avery nodded, reaching for a coffee cup. "Surprisingly after last night, and I'm looking forward to this morning, so thank you for the suggestion."

"And for insisting?" Marla asked wryly, but didn't wait for an answer. "I've eaten already, and so has the cat, but relax a minute with your coffee and breakfast. I'll meet you at the barn. I've settled on the grey gelding. Who do you want to ride?"

"The sorrel mare, Rosie."

"Good choice."

Avery was grateful for the breezy tone of Marla's voice. The combined aroma of coffee and food had her settling in her chair with a sense of contentment, until she noticed Callahan staring at her intently. He meowed. Loudly. She glanced at the plate Marla had used for him, but all that was left were bits of crust from his sandwich and the water bowl was full so his problem was neither hunger or thirst.

"What's up, Callahan?"

His next effort was almost a yowl but he wasn't making any move toward the door so she wasn't sure what he wanted her to do. "I don't have a clue what you want, but I'm trying, honest."

Callahan flattened his ears and glared at her. Sighing at the vagaries of male creatures, Avery finished her breakfast and slipped into her boots but when she reached the door, Callahan swatted at her jeans-clad leg.

"Hey! What's up with you, mister?" She reached down to rub his ears and found her hand clasped between the cat's front paws. His claws were sheathed but his pull was insistent.

"Come on, now, Callahan. I need this time off. You know as well as I do that Camp will keep things safe here."

Avery wasn't much surprised when Callahan wove his way between her legs with nearly every stride as she walked across the yard. She was unsure of the reason for his distress but he clearly *was* distressed about something. Perhaps no more than the fact that she was going to be out of his sight and protection this morning. She didn't have a doubt that he'd understood enough of their conversation to know. He was that kind of cat.

When she reached the barn, Marla had both horses saddled and was standing with them at the front of Barn Three. Out of habit, Avery checked her own tack and found everything impeccably in order as she expected. The sight of the rifle slid solidly into the scabbard gave her pause. "Firearms, Marla? We'll be on ranch property the whole time."

"I'm not taking any chances." Marla's voice was firm.

"Too much has happened."

At her feet, Callahan yowled again and snagged a paw firmly into the leather of her boot. Avery looked down. "Let go, Callahan. We won't leave this property, honest." She sighed as she looked back at Marla. "Okay, then, let's move. Where did you want to go?"

Marla's shoulders relaxed. "I thought we'd ride the perimeter then end at the twisted oak on the far end, maybe eat lunch under the small grove there. We've had enough rain this summer that the spring should be plenty deep with fresh water for the horses. I've packed a couple bottles of water and sandwiches for us."

* * *

I must find Camp. Something is very wrong. There are rifles attached to both saddles but I also glimpsed what appeared to be a handgun in the bag of food Marla packed before Avery exited her room. That is a lot of firepower for two women on what is supposed to be a leisurely ride. Maybe I've overlooked something, maybe we all have. Or maybe Marla is being overly cautious. All I know is, I don't like this turn of events.

* * *

Camp stood in the doorway of the guest house and watched the two women ride out. He didn't care for the fact that they were headed out alone, but he was smart enough to know he couldn't prevent it. Even so, he wasn't surprised when Callahan came yowling to his doorway and slipped inside.

Pouring another cup of coffee, Camp returned to his

laptop. He hadn't slept well and had been up for a while digging through the accumulation of information he'd received that morning.

He tried to ignore the cat pacing at his feet, but Callahan wasn't about to be disregarded. Camp gathered up his laptop and papers. "Come on, Mister. Let's at least get outside." After a moment's hesitation, he headed to Avery's side garden and the comfortable double glider.

For a moment, he allowed himself to focus on his memory of her sitting there the evening before, the late sunlight picking up the lighter tones through the curls that tumbled to her shoulder, catching on the brilliant green of her eyes. "Man," he said softly to himself, "you're hooked." That much, he knew was true, and as soon as he had sorted out the problems in her life and ensured her safety, he was going to do something about the fact. Maybe she didn't want another man in her life after all she'd been through, but he was damned if he'd walk away without trying.

He settled on the glider, wishing she were beside him. Callahan continued to pace, frequently swatting at his leg in a frustrated attempt to communicate his desire for Camp to take some action. The problem was Camp didn't know what action he was supposed to take.

The report on Neal Tarent proved him a non-starter, plenty of shady dealings in and out of the show-ring but more swagger and bluff and underhanded *money talks* deals than anything else.

He read, re-read, and filed a few more reports before hitting one with the handwriting analysis he'd requested. A keen sense of satisfaction came with the verification that Avery's signature conclusively did not match that on the checks she had purportedly signed. They were close but not close enough. To his surprise, however, Eddie Danson's also did not match. That information was completely unexpected, and he wasn't sure what to make of it. He filed that document away as well.

The next report was filled with photographs of Eddie Danson. There were a multitude of them over recent months and he scanned through cursorily. Then one brought his scrolling to a complete stop. It was at the local casino and the photograph was circled in bold red as were the next few. The researcher had realized quickly that the photographs were not of the same person. This Eddie Danson, impeccably dressed in what Camp felt certain was a name brand sports coat and derby hat, looked much younger, though the features seemed uncannily similar. At least what Camp could see of them. None of the circled photographs had caught him facing the camera. Did Danson have a son or a younger brother? No one had mentioned those possibilities to him, not here at New Hope or during the course of his investigation. Why hadn't he thought to ask? Avery had told him Marla didn't have any family besides her father, but maybe she didn't know. Damn it! He wished he'd dug a little deeper.

Camp stood abruptly, paced, tried not to step on Callahan who remained determined to get him to do something. He returned to study the photographs again, one at a time. There were several, all from casino security. One had been taken of what appeared to be a private card game, several of patrons at a black jack table, and one or two of a packed bar.

Camp felt a prickle along his neck. He didn't know the man, but he'd seen that face. He entered Avery's house without hesitation, searching for the calendar of ranch photographs they'd all admired last night. He found it on the counter and flipped to the month of September, of Marla with her hair pulled back and up and tucked under a fedora, her face little more than a profile, turned away from the camera. The barest glimpse, all he could see, of a strong jawline without the softening effect of hair swirling around her jaw and neck. A dark, arched eyebrow. What little was visible anyway. For whatever reason, the women had preferred the horses, not themselves, to be the focal points of the photography.

Not a son or a brother. Marla.

Camp pulled his cell phone from his pocket and hit Avery's number. The call went straight to voice mail. His gaze moved to Callahan who had followed him in, undoubtedly anxious and trying his best to get Camp to understand what the cat had clearly already deduced.

"Can you find them?"

Callahan meowed sharply and turned, heading toward the door, obviously satisfied now that Camp had shown himself ready to take action.

Camp made only one stop. To grab his rifle from behind the seat of his truck.

* * *

I hope Camp can keep up with me. I'm sure of our destination but we'll have to take a short cut over some tricky territory to be there ahead of Avery and Marla. Fortunately, Camp's exercise routine is daily and strenuous—he's no shirker—and he has a partiality for loaded firearms that he carries concealed at all times, one at his shoulder, one at his ankle. The rifle he retrieved is lagniappe, *just that little* something extra.

My fear is that we may not reach Avery in time. I'm not sure of all the implications, but clearly Camp was disturbed by the picture of Marla. It's enough for me to know that it's from Marla that Avery must be protected. The whys and wherefores can come later. Time is critical.

* * *

The morning proved absolutely beautiful, and Avery felt a peace she hadn't enjoyed in some time. The horses were content to walk when the path was uncertain and trot or slow gallop when the ground was flat. Avery let Marla choose the pace.

"Let me know if you get ready to stop," Marla said to her. "If you get tired."

Avery shot her an amused look. "We've been riding … what? … a couple of hours and walked as much as anything. This is hardly the pace of our normal day. What about you? Holding up okay?"

Marla rolled her eyes. "You've got to quit worrying."

"I can't shake the realization that I nearly lost you, that you could have been killed in that car wreck. I don't want you to push yourself."

"We've both been pushing ourselves for a while," Marla said dryly.

"That reminds me of something I was considering earlier. I think it's time we thought about adding full-time barn help or doubling our part-time crew. I see plenty of benefits to permanent positions because that would give us an eventual knowledge base for backup and possible training as fill-in instructors."

Marla pondered that a moment. "On the other hand,

we've been able to help some bright kids get through college without an overload of debt with our part-time work."

"Exactly. And I hate to lose that aspect."

Marla swatted at a horsefly aggravating her young mount. "What if we mix the ideas? Alan will graduate this semester. What if we take his opening and make one permanent position and keep the other two as part-time for now?"

"I like that. It would give us a chance to see how the full-time will work out."

Marla swatted again. "Let's speed up a bit, put them into an extended trot and see if we can shake some of these horseflies."

Avery pressed her heels lightly but firmly into Rosie's sides as Marla gave a quiet verbal command to the young grey she was riding. When the terrain grew rocky, they pulled back to a walk, but Avery was pleased to note the tactic to leave the irritating insects behind seemed to have worked, at least for now.

They walked the horses in silence, each lost to their thoughts, as the hills leveled and the stand of oaks that was their destination became a haze of green on the horizon.

Avery hadn't realized that Marla had fallen behind her until she spoke again, so quietly and evenly the words didn't make sense until Avery glanced back and saw the pistol Marla held trained at her back. "What? What did you say?"

"I said I killed Missy. My mother, too."

For a moment Avery didn't, couldn't, speak. Her mind couldn't comprehend. "Your sister drowned."

Marla's expression was serene. They could as easily have been talking about the weather or the ranch. The pistol in Marla's hand was steady—and so was her gaze on Avery's face. Waves of cold swept over Avery. Mind racing, she fought not to let it show. No weakness, she thought, I mustn't show weakness, though she didn't know why not or what difference it could make.

"Missy did drown, yes. I always made sure she was safely seat-belted into her wheelchair. It was my job. Mom said so. Couldn't have her falling out and getting hurt. So, I double-checked that she was securely strapped in when I slipped up behind her to unlock the wheels." The corner of Marla's mouth lifted in a slight smile. "Missy never heard me, never knew I was there, until I gave her chair a push toward the pool. She opened her mouth to cry out, but I said her name. When she turned and saw me, I said, 'I've got you, Missy. It's okay.'"

Marla paused and Avery heard the call of a bird, the rustle of a rabbit in the brush close by. "And you drowned her." Even as Avery said the words, she couldn't believe them. Not yet.

"It wasn't hard. Missy trusted me so she didn't call for mom, who was asleep anyway. I'd already sneaked into the house and made sure of that. I was right there, after all. I always had her. When I jumped into the water, Missy thought I was coming to save her. It was easy to hold the wheelchair down long enough for her lungs to fill with water. She watched me, every second, there under the water. Just watched me. After that, all I had to do was 'find' her when I came in from ball practice. I did the hysterical thing really well ... seems I have a talent for acting." That half smile reappeared fleetingly then Marla's expression turned remote, unemotional, a look Avery had seen on many occasions and failed to interpret.

Avery was hit by waves of nausea. "Why? Why would you do that? How could you kill your own sister?"

Marla lifted one shoulder. "She took up too much of Mom's time. There was so much I wanted to do, places I wanted to go, but there was always Missy, her disability, in the way. Missy was okay, but she was weak. She couldn't help it, of course, but I can't stand weakness. That's why I always liked you. You were strong."

"And your mother?" Avery watched her as she would a rattlesnake, a creature cold and deadly and completely devoid of humanity.

"Mom was even weaker than Missy but in a different way. Drank herself into a stupor every night after Missy died—all because she'd fallen asleep on the sunporch with Missy still outside by the pool. She thought if Missy needed anything, she'd hear her and wake up." Marla shrugged. "I'm sure she would have but I couldn't very well tell her that. She couldn't bear the guilt, and I couldn't take it from her."

"So, it wasn't suicide."

"I'm sure Mom wanted to die. She even told me that once. And she would have drunk herself to death eventually. So, I guess you could say it was suicide, just daughter-assisted."

"And you're planning to kill me because….?"

"Oh, I'm not planning to kill you. I *have* to kill you. And don't even think about the rifle in your scabbard. Yours isn't loaded. Mine is."

"But why me? Why now? I don't understand. Marla, everything I have would have been yours." Avery couldn't wrap her mind around anything Marla had said. The sounds of nature around them that had sounded so sweet minutes ago now seemed a mockery.

"And so it will be—just sooner. I'd planned to wait awhile longer, but you and Mr. Kirkland are getting much too cozy. Do you think I haven't noticed? Besides, you've kept way too close an eye on things since you found out Dad was cheating you, and I can't be sure you won't eventually figure out I was too. And if you don't, Camp Kirkland will. He's smart, too smart. I can't risk you changing your will if that happens. I've worked too hard for this place; I've earned it."

"You asked me to change my will." Avery felt as if she'd fallen down the rabbit hole with Alice in Wonderland, into a world where absolutely nothing made sense. She struggled to make logic of what she was seeing and hearing in a person she thought she knew as well as she knew her own self.

"Well, yes, but I knew you'd never do that. I wanted you to believe I'd give up everything to keep you safe … until I was ready. I need Dad out of the way and soon. He's no use to me now that you're divorced. He's made a complete mess of things and is way over his head in debt. I'm not about to bail him out or keep listening to his whining."

"His gambling debts, you mean."

"Yes, and how dumb is that? I like to gamble, too, seems to be the one thing we have in common these days, but I don't drink when I gamble and I don't gamble with sharks. All my debt is in his name. So poor Dad is in way too deep with men too smart for him to handle and those guys are going to keep on making trouble until he's out of the way for good. I thought they'd take care of that for me, but now they've turned their attention to the ranch and the horses. Can't have that now, can I?"

She sounded indignant, Avery thought, feeling as if she were caught in some nightmare. Marla was actually indignant that her father hadn't been murdered by thugs to keep her from having to do it. Avery felt sickened at the realization that she had completely missed the fact that Marla lacked the ability to care about any human, even those closest to her.

"On top of all that, you and Leanne keep pouring the ranch resources into rescue horses and then giving them away. That's not good business. Anyway, it makes more sense to kill you, now that I've got it all worked out."

"What? What have you got worked out?"

Marla looked at her as if she were simple-minded. "Dad calls me for help almost every day. This time I told him to meet me here, and I'd help him a little. Sadly, he's going to shoot your horse out from under you and you'll hit your head on some rock or break your neck or something. I'll figure that out before we get to the oak grove. I'll have to kill him trying to save you, but—oh, so sad—his death will be in vain as you'll be beyond saving. Your part's easy. All you have to do is keep riding. Dad won't be along for another little while, but you'll be dead by then."

Avery looked toward the oak trees growing ever nearer and tried her best to marshal her thoughts. She was alone and without a weapon, but she'd be damned if she'd die without a fight.

Chapter 18

Ahead of us are the oak trees that I believe to be Marla's destination. The site doesn't look threatening, just a small grove with one very old, very large oak among the several younger ones. Although I'm edgy over what lies ahead of us, I'm pretty pleased with Camp. We've managed to arrive ahead of Avery and what may prove to be the evil stepdaughter. Camp has proven himself a man of strength and stamina. It helped that we could take a more direct route than the horses, though it involved Camp scaling a few fences and fording a few rocky streams.

Now, Avery must prove herself a female of fortitude and ingenuity and keep herself safe until we get in place. Without a doubt she'll need both in the moments ahead if this mess isn't to end in disaster.

* * *

Camp scrambled up the oddly shaped branches of the largest tree behind Callahan, praying that Avery and Marla were too far distant to discern any real movement around the copse of oaks. His pulse thudded, minute by minute, as they drew closer. He recognized the primal fear that gripped him. Avery was his to protect, and he was terrified that every bit of strength and knowledge and skill he could claim might not be enough to save her.

Taking a deep breath, he put that terror aside and watched the approach of the two women. Avery rode at the front. Marla followed close behind. The sun glinted on the pistol in Marla's hand, and Camp's gut clenched. He hadn't been mistaken then. Unlikely as it had seemed, Marla—not her father—was the danger that threatened Avery.

Camp had a choice to make. Ease the rifle into position and risk a distance shot with Avery riding in front of Marla or secure the rifle and ensure his pistol was at the ready. Either carried a peril. Any animal was subject to an unexpected movement and young horses particularly so. Once he pulled the trigger, if Avery's sorrel shifted the slightest in the wrong direction, she could be placed in the path of the bullet he released. Waiting until they were within pistol range would leave Avery at Marla's mercy that much longer, and he had no way to be sure this small thicket of trees was even their final direction although Callahan had led the way and seemed sure that it was.

In the end, Camp decided to trust whatever instinct or knowledge had steered the cat to this spot. The cat had been dead-on so far. Camp held his breath and eased his pistol from its holster. Sweat that had nothing to do with the heat trickled down his forehead as he watched their slow approach. He sensed, rather than heard, Callahan shift position as the women neared their hiding place and prayed that neither of them would notice. If Avery felt their presence and glanced up, Marla's gaze would follow hers, and Camp had no earthly idea how she might react at that point.

Avery stared back the way they'd ridden. "I don't see your father."

Camp tensed. Was Eddie part of this after all? Camp couldn't risk looking around for him. Not now when Avery and Marla were so close to the tree where he and Callahan waited.

"Well, I don't actually need him here right now." Marla hesitated, seeming to weigh her options. "Besides, he's such a loser I can't even be sure he'll show up."

Camp saw her grip shift, tighten on the pistol. Avery must have seen it as well. In a move that startled Marla as much as it did him, Avery kicked her feet free of the stirrups, slapped her mount on the neck and leapt for Marla's horse, all in one swift act of desperation.

Forced to hold his shot, Camp dropped from the tree, landing hard on his feet in the same moment a yowling gray cat dropped from the limb beside him to land squarely on the hip of Marla's horse.

As her panicked mount whirled at the weight of the cat and the feel of claws digging into tender hide, Marla's shot went wild, and she growled with rage. Before she could fire a second time, Camp grabbed her arm, dragging her from the horse. She tumbled to the ground, and her pistol fell and discharged again. Camp could only pray that shot, too, went wide of any mark. With a rough twist of her shoulder, he pinned her—face down with her arms pulled behind her—and planted a knee in her back. Not until then, with heart still thudding, could he let his gaze find Avery.

She had landed on her rear a few feet away. For long moments, they simply stared at each other as both horses bolted away from the sound and smell of gunfire and one unleashed cat.

Callahan sat guard between Marla and her pistol and, at this point, Camp couldn't be sure the cat wasn't capable of using it.

"Get the pistol, Avery." It was all Camp could trust himself to say for a moment.

For answer, Avery scrambled to her feet, dusting the back of her jeans. She rubbed the fur between Callahan's ears before picking up the gun.

Only when Camp saw the pistol secure in her hand, did he ask, "Do you have your cell phone?"

Avery gestured in the direction the terrified horses had fled. "I'd say it's about halfway back to the barn."

"Then come get mine and call Tucker, then Farley."

As she walked toward him, Camp let himself breathe a sigh of relief. Avery was safe. They'd sort the rest out, but—for now—that was all that was important, all that mattered.

Not even Marla's shrieks and curses bothered him at this point.

* * *

The days came and went, turned into a week and then another. Avery worked and grieved and healed. Camp had left her with a kiss and a promise that he'd be back, but she wasn't sure how she felt about that. She wasn't sure how she felt about anything. He called her each night, sent her a text each morning, and still she didn't know, wasn't sure. They'd actually known each other such a short while, a matter of days, really, before it had been time for him to leave. Was that enough?

"Avery?" At the sound of her name, she glanced over her shoulder. Leanne stood at the entrance of the barn, watching as she ran a brush lovingly over Jack's gleaming neck. "Ben—Sheriff Farley—drove out to see you. Do you want me to send him in here?"

"No, I'll come out. I'm done." She gave Jack a hug and led him back into the stall before slipping the halter from his head. It was the horses, Leanne and Tucker, the ranch itself, the work she believed in, that brought the healing she needed.

But she missed Camp. Little as she liked it, as uncomfortable as it made her, she couldn't deny the fact.

The sheriff waited beside his truck. He'd placed his hat on the hood and the dry September breeze ruffled his silvering hair. "Avery." He studied her closely. "You look good. Rested."

He'd been present, witnessed as his men had loaded a handcuffed Marla into the back of a patrol car. He'd watched as tears of shock and disbelief had slid down Avery's cheeks.

"I'm better," Avery said, smiling at him, "but I don't know about rested. It's been busy around here." And without Marla they were short-handed, but Avery wasn't ready to add anyone to their team. Not yet, not this soon. She'd have to eventually, she knew, but bringing someone into their day-to-day lives was an important choice, and they'd make it together, she and Tucker and Leanne

"What brings you out this way?" Though she suspected she knew and dreaded to hear.

"I've got news of Marla. Thought it best to tell you face-to-face."

Avery braced herself and waited.

Ben Farley sighed. "She waived all rights and refused a court-appointed attorney. Told the judge every detail of what she'd done and what she planned to do. And showed no remorse or shame or even a hint of emotion for any of it. It beat all I've ever seen, Avery."

"But they judged her as insane, right?"

The sheriff shook his head. "No, Avery, they didn't. She still might plead for that and might even get it, but for now, she's moving through the system. She'll have her day in court before it's finished, but ..." He sighed. "When it's all said and done, I expect she'll get one life sentence for murdering her twin and another for murdering her mother. There'll be other charges, of course, attempted murder..." he let his voice trail away.

"I'll never understand," Avery whispered.

"No, ma'am, me nor you. She was a cool one, all along, could have been killed when she rolled that SUV."

Avery looked startled. "What do you mean?"

"There was a witness, a hired heavy on a bike trailing her and thinking it was you, planning who-knows-what to get a payoff for his boss. Camp put me on to him, but it took a while for me to track him down. He was willing enough to talk when I did, as long as it was off the record. Said Marla was alone on the road ahead of him. No one forced her off."

"That's insane."

"Crazy business every bit of it," Ben agreed. "He also understands there's not a single good reason for him to be hanging around this part of the country. And every reason not to. Speaking of which, have you heard anything from her dad?"

"Eddie? No, I haven't and don't expect to."

"I heard he lit out after Marla was arrested. Guess he's still running from his debt, but at least you won't be bothered over that again. Camp Kirkland and I made enough visits in uniform to be sure of that."

"Camp?"

Ben looked at her quizzically. "You didn't know?"

"Seems like every time I turn around there's something I don't know."

"Well, looks like I stepped my shoe in it this time, but I'll leave the explanations to him." Ben gave her a hug before getting into his truck. "You call if you need me, Avery, any time day or night."

"I'll be fine."

Ben smiled as he closed his door. "I expect you will, at that."

She watched the sheriff pull out of the drive before turning back to her work, nearly stepping on Callahan in the process. She scooped him up and rubbed her face against his soft fur. "You saved my life. I'll never forget that."

* * *

Why, yes, I did. Me and Camp, who is long overdue for return. And that needs to be soon, as I suspect Dax will get the urge to move on before too much longer. Though the danger has passed, Avery still needs me close at her side. She doesn't wake us both crying out in her sleep now, but her dreams are restless and her heart needs attention that only a human, a human who loves her, can give. I'm a poor substitute for Camp, but I'm all she has for the moment.

I know Dax understands. I've made sure to check in with him each evening, but he knows I return here to sleep close to Avery until Camp returns.

I've made sure to spend time with young Tucker as well. He fancied himself in love with Marla, and he's looked nothing but sad these past few weeks. Avery tries to comfort him but she needs as much as she gives there. Such a pity. I've heard the term heartless. Even used it a few times. I've met criminals with an evil heart. But never before have I met a human, like Marla, who had none at all.

* * *

It was time to convene a meeting of her team, Avery decided. Past time. A month had come and gone since Marla had exited their lives in a way none could have foreseen. A month since she'd seen Camp. A month to pull herself together. Now it was time to be there, to be present, for her team.

At the end of the work day, they gathered in her garden. She with a glass of wine, Tucker with a beer, and Leanne with a tumbler of iced tea. Callahan shared the double glider with her, and she kept it moving gently because that was what he liked.

Avery took a breath and jumped right in. "I'm doubling our part-time barn help. We'll have one morning, one afternoon student for each barn. I contacted the school and they're going to send us the applications and resumes of the students who are interested. I'll need you to look through those." She shifted her gaze to Tucker and smiled. "It's also time to start building the clinic. Dr. Snow called me yesterday. He's planning to retire next summer. He has someone to take on his small animal practice but would like to send his equine clients here, to you."

Tucker looked shellshocked but only for a moment before he grinned broadly. It was his first real smile since Marla's arrest.

"Which," Leanne inserted, "means we'll need to start looking for someone to manage Barn Two."

"It does, yes, and I'll need both of you heavily invested in that selection process. We're a team, and we're going to want to bring in someone with the same mindset. I'm also going to begin looking for someone to take over the accounts. I do it well enough, I suppose, but it isn't what I love and I can't manage it and my barn as well."

Her gaze went to Leanne as she spoke.

"You already know," Leanne said accusingly.

"Perhaps," Avery admitted, rubbing a hand along Callahan's back. "But you could tell us."

Leanne laughed. "Well, we don't know the sex but arrival will be mid-March."

Tucker hooted. "We're having a baby? Awesome! Uncle Tucker. Sounds good, right?"

"It does." Leanne leaned her head into his shoulder. "Uncle Tucker."

"And so …?" Avery prompted.

"And so, at some point soon, I'll need to slow down, for a while at least, which means I could take over the books then. But we'll for sure need someone to be ready to take my place once the baby is here. I'm not a bookkeeper at heart either."

"It will take a bit of juggling but we'll work it out. I'll start talking with some of the colleges for prospects as well as place an ad or two in some of the journals we subscribe to."

They talked until nearly dark, and it felt good to be making plans, to be looking forward instead of behind. Leanne drove away toward her home with Jason, and Tucker drifted back to the bunkhouse, but Avery continued to swing and sip a second glass of wine.

It felt almost as if she'd been expecting the headlights that turned into the long drive. Callahan seemed to be as well, purring against her hand but not bothering to come to attention as he eyed the sweep of light along the neat fences before the truck parked.

Avery stayed where she was, watching as Camp walked toward her. He stopped, seeming to drink in the sight of her as much as she was of him. He held an envelope toward her.

"The acceptance of New Hope Ranch into the veterans' equine rehab program."

She took it without speaking, turning it in her hand. The program, her acceptance, was still important to her, but not, she thought, nearly as important as this man standing in front of her.

Searching her eyes with his gaze, Camp held out his hand to her and she took it. She allowed him to tug her to her feet, and—without hesitation—she stepped into his arms.

Chapter 19

Just after dawn with her first cup of coffee poured and sitting on the counter, Avery opened the garden door to a polite rap on the frame. She gave a soft, unhappy sigh at the sight of Dax with Callahan at his heels.

"So soon?"

"Yes, ma'am, been here longer than most places. Callahan wasn't ready 'til now." He glanced at the cat at his feet before handing her the list she'd given him that first day. "All finished."

"And perfectly done, according to my team." She hated to see them go. "There's always a list of things here waiting for someone to have time. Some long term. As a matter of fact, I'm going to need someone to manage the building of a veterinary clinic here, from the ground up." Dax would be perfect in that role, she thought. And, it would keep the burden from Tucker who could be free to make design and aesthetic decisions but not tied to overseeing the work and managing county inspections. She had no doubt that Dax would ensure no corners were cut in material and installation. And it would keep Dax—and Callahan—close.

"I appreciate, ma'am, I do, but I'm not much for management."

"I'd have to disagree." A man able to manage his own time, always knew how best to manage the time of others. And one capable of doing everything that needed doing, would always know when someone else was doing it correctly. And when they were not.

But Avery could tell by the look on his face—pleased by the compliment but not tempted by the offer—that she wouldn't be able to persuade him.

Callahan brushed against her legs, and she gathered him up in a hug, her face touching his. Her gaze met Dax's. "Will you at least stop back if you find yourself this way again?"

"Yes, ma'am, Callahan and I will make a promise to you on that."

Avery reluctantly handed the cat to him and watched as he settled Callahan atop his backpack, paws resting on broad shoulders.

* * *

Time now for the next leg of our journey. I'll miss Avery and her team, but I find Camp to be a fitting mate for this strong woman. They'll take care of each other. I can leave here with a good conscience, knowing that I leave the security of New Hope Ranch in very capable hands.

Thank you for taking the time to read *Callahan and the Horses of Hope*. If you enjoyed it, please consider telling your friends or posting a short review. Word of mouth is an author's best friend and is much appreciated.

Thank you!
Susan

* * *

Also by Susan Yawn Tanner
The Cat Callahan Mystery Series
(with Rebecca Barrett):
Callahan on the Case
Callahan and the Horses of Hope
Callahan's Christmas Feast (short story)
A Callahan Christmas (short story)

The Bellamys of Texas historical romance series:
Winds Across Texas
Fire Across Texas
Storm Out of Texas

The Bellamy Legacy contemporary romance series:
A Dangerous Inheritance

The Scottish Highlands Romances
Highland Captive
Captive to a Dream
Exiled Heart

A Warm Southern Christmas
(a historical romance novella)

Susan Yawn Tanner is a bestselling author in the romance and mystery genres. When she isn't writing, she's either tending her horses or barrel racing. Although she lives less than an hour from the Gulf of Mexico, the white sandy beaches of Mississippi can't compete with the lure of arena dirt.

Scan the QR code or visit the website to sign up for Susan's newsletter where she announces new books and exciting giveaways.

susanytanner.com

Made in the USA
Coppell, TX
14 June 2025